ALL SHE EVER DREAMED

BOULDER CREEK ROMANCE
BOOK TWO

ROBIN LEE HATCHER

Paperback ISBN: 978-1-7372845-8-1
eBook ISBN: 978-1-7372845-9-8

Library of Congress Control Number: 2022919577

Published by RobinSong, Inc.
Meridian, Idaho

PROLOGUE

Cuba, July 1898

The Stars and Stripes fluttered in the hot breeze above the captured trenches of San Juan Hill. Jeremiah West, his thigh bleeding, dropped to the ground beside the other Rough Riders and doughboys, all of them panting and sweating. Numbly, he looked back at the way they'd come.

The wounded and dead littered the slope. Everywhere, Spaniards and Americans lay in pools of their own blood. A gray haze hung over the earth, and Jeremiah's nostrils burned with the acrid scent of gun smoke. A humming sound filled his ears. The moans of the wounded. There had to be a thousand of them.

He caught sight of the colonel standing over a Spaniard's body and knew Roosevelt was reveling in the victory and the gore. Jeremiah had expected to feel the same. He didn't. Instead, he felt empty, the same haunting emptiness he'd felt for years.

A voice whispered in his heart, *Go home, Jeremiah. It's time you went home.*

Yes. It was time. Finally, he would go home again.

CHAPTER
ONE

Boulder Creek, Idaho, December 1898

B undled against the frigid day, Sarah McNeal hurried along the boardwalk toward the train station. Her younger brother was due to arrive today, and she needed to be there when he stepped off the train. Tom had been away at boarding school for three years, but it seemed longer to Sarah. She missed him more than she'd expected. And come spring he would leave again, this time for Boston where he would begin his medical training. The next time he returned to Boulder Creek, he would be a doctor.

How proud she was at that thought. Her brother, a physician. Tom was young—only eighteen—and already he was on his way to achieving something meaningful, something he'd dreamed about since he was a boy. She envied him.

When she stepped onto the depot platform, she saw Doc Varney standing close to the building, out of the icy wind that stung her cheeks. She raised her hand and waved.

Doctor Kevin Varney was a distinguished looking man with

3

glasses, gray hair, and a bushy beard. It was he who'd encouraged Tom to pursue higher education so he could practice medicine. Many were the nights when her brother, only eleven or twelve at the time, had gone to Doc Varney's home. He'd studied the medical books that lined the doctor's shelves and had asked the older man question upon question. The physician had been impressed by Tom's intelligence and eagerness to learn, and he'd gone to great lengths to help her brother be admitted to the Elias Crane Science Academy for Boys in San Francisco. Sarah would always be grateful for his kindness.

"I didn't know you'd be here," she said as she stopped beside the doctor.

He smiled at her. "Not come and welcome Tom home? You know me better than that, young lady." His expression sobered. "How's your grandfather?"

"Ornery as ever. It was all I could do to make him wait at home. He kept saying a little fresh air would be good for him."

"Catch pneumonia is what he'd do." The doctor tugged at the collar of his coat. "I can't say the two of us won't do the same."

She nodded in agreement, then gazed down the length of track that stretched toward the southeast end of the valley. She hoped the train would be on time. If it was even a few minutes late, her grandfather might disobey her orders and come to the station after all.

Hank McNeal, at seventy-four, was as strong-willed as he'd ever been. It was only his body that had weakened. At one time a tall, barrel-chested man, he was now much thinner and somewhat bent with age. He lacked the energy that used to carry him through each day. Still, he refused to retire from his position as sheriff. Sarah had been after him for months to hire a deputy, but so far, according to her grandfather, he hadn't found anyone suitable.

After Sarah's grandmother—Hank's wife of fifty-one years —passed away the previous summer, it had become Sarah's responsibility to make sure her grandfather got the rest he needed. That was never an easy task. Perhaps he would be better behaved while Tom was home. After all, her brother would be a doctor one day. Grandpa would have to listen to him. Wouldn't he?

"There she comes," Doc Varney said.

Sarah focused her gaze once again on the ribbon of track. She saw the billowing cloud of soot shooting into the air moments before the engine came into view. Her excitement surged to the fore once again.

"Do you suppose he's changed much?" She rose on tiptoe, her eagerness making it difficult to stand still.

"Of course he's changed. He left a boy. He's coming home a man."

Doc Varney was right. Tom McNeal *had* become a man. Sarah almost didn't recognize him when he stepped down from the train ten minutes later. Taller by a good eight inches or more and sporting a mustache, Tom looked up and down the platform before his gaze came to rest upon her.

She rushed forward and threw herself into his arms. "Tommy!" She gave him a kiss on the cheek, then stepped back. "Look at you!"

"Like it?" Wearing a cocky grin, he turned his head so she could view the mustache from another angle.

She frowned. "I'm not sure."

Doc Varney stepped up behind her. "I like it, young man. Gives you a look of distinction." He held out his hand. "Welcome home."

"Thank you, sir." Tom shook the older man's hand.

"I've heard good reports about you," the doctor continued, his voice oddly gruff.

"I've done my best, sir."

"I knew you would." Doc Varney cleared his throat as he released Tom's hand. "I won't keep you. It's too blasted cold to stand about, and your grandfather's anxious to see you. When you get settled, come to my office and we'll have a long visit."

"I'll do it."

Sarah slipped her arm through her brother's. "You're home. I can't believe it. You're finally home."

Tom looked at her again, and his grin returned. "You got even prettier. No wonder Warren's been pestering you to marry him." He shook his head. "It's hard to believe you'll be a married woman in a few weeks."

It was hard for her to believe, too, and she'd rather not think about it. Thoughts of her impending wedding left her feeling unsettled.

Her brother tapped the end of her nose with a gloved finger. "And I always thought you'd wait for that English lord to ride in on his white horse."

She playfully slapped his shoulder, then smiled as she tugged on his arm. "Let's go home. Grandpa can't wait to see you, and I've got lunch ready for you both. I made all your favorites. I know you must be hungry after your long journey."

"You bet I am. Just let me get my luggage."

As Tom turned to pick up his bags, Sarah noticed a man standing in the passenger car doorway. His face was obscured by the deep shadows of the car, yet she sensed he watched her, had been watching for some time. A shiver ran up her spine.

"I'm ready," Tom said, abruptly pulling her attention back to him. "Let's go eat that feast you've worked so hard preparing for your little brother."

JEREMIAH FELT A STING OF ENVY AS HE WATCHED THE JUBILANT homecoming. No one would be on the platform to welcome him back to Boulder Creek the way that young man had been welcomed. Of course, no one knew Jeremiah was coming, but he doubted things would have been different even if he'd sent word ahead.

Hunching his shoulders inside his coat, he stepped to the platform, walked the length of it, then stared toward the center of town. Boulder Creek had changed in the many years he'd been away. He shouldn't be surprised, but he was. Instead of a single street, the town had several. New houses and businesses had sprouted up. From where he stood, he saw a second church at the opposite end of town. There was even a hotel and a bank.

Have I done the right thing coming back?

He turned toward the train again and went after his belongings. There wasn't much. He'd packed everything he owned into a couple of carpetbags. He hoisted them, one in each hand, and headed into town.

Snow crunched beneath his boots as he made his way to Barber Mercantile. Four years ago, Sam Barber, the proprietor, had written to Jeremiah to tell him of his father's death. The news had killed his dreams of ever finding a way to prove himself to his father. Perhaps that was why the rest of Mr. Barber's letter had surprised him. His father's will had left the farm to Jeremiah. Even now, it was difficult to believe. Why him and not his younger brother? Perhaps Sam's wife, Emma, would be able to answer that question. As he recalled, Mrs. Barber knew everything about everybody in the valley.

A bell chimed above his head as he opened the door to the store. A wave of nostalgia washed over him at the familiar sights and smells. The town might be different, but nothing had changed in this establishment. He could have been a kid again, stopping by the mercantile on his way home from school. He knew where the pickle barrel would be and the jar of licorice, too.

A woman behind the counter turned from the shelves. She was too young to be Emma Barber, yet there was something familiar about her.

"Hello. May I help you?" she asked.

He set his carpetbags on the floor near the door, then removed his hat as he strode forward. "I'm looking for Sam Barber."

"I'm sorry." She shook her head. "Mr. Barber died almost two years ago. Is there something—" She stopped and stared. "Why, you're Jeremiah West." She placed a hand on her collarbone. "I'm Leslie. Leslie Barber. Well, it's Leslie Blake now. I don't suppose you remember me at all. I was a child when you went away. How long has it been?"

"Close to fourteen years."

"Land o' Goshen! Is it really? I can hardly believe it. You must not recognize the town. Boulder Creek isn't like it used to be when we were children. The railroad's come through and we've got our own hotel and that new Methodist Church. The school's about bursting at the seams, what with all the children everybody's got. I was saying to Annalee... You remember my sister, don't you? Well, I was saying to her the other day how much everything's changed. We've watched it happen, but it must be a real surprise to someone who's been away as long as you."

It wasn't so much that he remembered Leslie as that she reminded him of her mother. Plump and warm-natured, Emma Barber had loved to chatter whenever someone was in the store, the same way Leslie was doing now.

Suddenly, she stopped, then said, "I'm real sorry about

your wife. And your pa. I lost both my parents. I know how it feels."

"Your ma's gone, too?"

Her voice lowered to a whisper. "Yes."

"I'm sorry to hear it. I remember her well. She was a kind woman."

The door joining the living quarters to the mercantile opened, drawing both their gazes.

"George, come here," Leslie called, her smile returning, although not as bright. "There's someone I'd like you to meet." As soon as the man was close enough, she reached out and took hold of his hand, then faced Jeremiah again. "This is my husband, George Blake. George, this is Jeremiah West, Warren's older brother."

George shook Jeremiah's hand. "Good to meet you."

He nodded his own greeting.

"Are you back to stay?" Leslie asked.

"Don't know for sure. I think so."

"Well, then. Tell us what you've been doing all these years."

What had he been doing? Running. Trying to forget. Staying alone so he wouldn't feel the loss—or the guilt. Living but not living.

He couldn't say any of that, but he might as well tell her what he could. Leslie wouldn't be the last person to ask the question. He'd better get used to it. "After Marta died, I moved around a lot. I worked cattle, did some bartending, even spent time with the railroad before going to work in a factory in New York City. Last couple of years, I was in the army."

"The army? Were you in the war?"

Scenes of the battlefield flashed in his head. "Yes. I was in the war."

"Were you hurt bad?" She glanced at his leg.

Hard as he tried to hide it, people noticed his limp. But he didn't want anyone's pity. Especially not in Boulder Creek. "No. Not bad." He put his hat on. "I'd better get over to the livery and see about renting a rig. Warren's not expecting me, and I need to get to the farm before dark."

Leslie shook her head. "You won't find your brother at the farm. He's got rooms above his carpentry shop, right down the street."

"A carpentry shop?"

"He makes furniture. Real good at it, too." She frowned. "He never mentioned you were coming home."

"He didn't know. We haven't been in touch."

He saw surprise flicker across her face, and he turned to leave the mercantile before she could ask more questions.

TWO

J eremiah read the sign above the shop: WEST CARPENTRY.
So this was his kid brother's place. It hadn't occurred to
him that Warren would do something besides work the
farm. But he supposed it was no more odd than their father
leaving the place to Jeremiah, the wayward son.

He opened the door to the shop and stepped inside. In the
dim light, he saw a man run a hand over the surface of a table
in the back of the long, narrow room.

"Be with you in a minute." His brother's voice had deep-
ened. Not unexpected after fourteen years. He'd been a skinny
youth back then. He was taller now, too. Probably as tall as
Jeremiah. Even bent over the table, his height was obvious.
This was not the boy of Jeremiah's memory.

He cleared his throat as he took a step deeper into the shop.

Warren turned and squinted.

Jeremiah supposed he was nothing but a dark silhouette
with the light from the windows at his back. "Hello, Warren."

The squint turned to a frown.

"Have I changed that much?"

The silence stretched into what felt like an eternity before Warren said, "Jeremiah?"

"Yeah. It's me. You've changed too."

"I didn't expect to ever see you again."

Jeremiah's gaze traveled around the shop, his eyes now adjusted to the dim light. "A business of your own. Dad must have been proud of you."

"I didn't have the shop until after he died." His brother took a step forward. "What brought you back to Boulder Creek?"

"It was time. I heard you're staying in town. Is there room for me at the farm?"

"The house is empty." A muscle flexed in his jaw. "I put the farm up for sale."

Jeremiah heard the challenge in Warren's voice and chose not to respond at once. Instead, he set his carpetbags on the floor and walked around the shop, stopping to run his fingers over the tables, bedsteads, and chairs that filled the room. When he'd come full circle, he faced his brother. "You can't sell the farm. It's legally mine. Dad left it to me."

"So what if he did? You weren't here. You never came back, never wrote. For all I knew, you were dead. That made it mine."

"I'm not dead."

"I need the money. I'm getting married in a few weeks."

"Married?"

"Yes." Warren spun around and walked to the table at the back of the shop. "Why'd you return?"

"Sorry it's inconvenienced you."

His brother didn't look at him.

Jeremiah drew a deep breath. "Tell you what. I'll pay you half what the property's worth. That should help set you up with your bride."

"You'd do that?"

"Yeah. I'd do that. Half the farm should have gone to you anyway."

"I guess that's fair. As fair as it could ever be."

SARAH CARRIED THE DISH OF STEAMING VEGETABLES INTO THE DINING room and set it in the center of the large table. "I'm sorry Warren couldn't join us for lunch, but he'll be here for supper."

"I don't mind having you and Grandpa to myself." Tom smiled at her. "Or the food to myself either. You don't know how much I missed home cooking. They didn't serve meals like this at the academy, I can promise you that."

The compliment warmed her heart. "Grandma taught me the best she could. I hope this is as good as hers." She settled onto her chair. "Why don't you say grace?"

Tom nodded, then bowed his head. "We thank You, Father, for bringing us back together. Bless this food You've provided from Your bounty. Amen."

"Amen," Sarah and Grandpa whispered in unison.

Tom glanced at them both, a mischievous glint in his eyes, then reached for the platter of roast beef. "I'm starved."

Sarah laughed. As a little boy, Tom had been constantly hungry. He'd pestered their grandmother for something to eat from the moment he woke up until it was time to go to bed. With those sweet memories playing in her head, she watched her brother heap mashed potatoes onto his plate. He might have changed in other ways, but his boyish appetite remained.

Grandpa accepted the platter from Tom. "This is a treat. Most days, Sarah brings lunch to the jail for me. Or for the deputy, when I have one. It's always good, but nothing like this. She's trying to spoil you, Tom."

"It's working." Her brother poured gravy over the generous portions of roast beef and potatoes on his plate.

Sarah beamed with pleasure.

Tom passed the gravy boat to Grandpa. "Did I tell you Dr. Crane visited me at the academy when he was in San Francisco? He told me all about the institute."

Grandpa shook his head. "No, you didn't tell us that."

"I've never met anyone like him. He's dynamic. Truly brilliant. He's the best teacher of medicine in the country. No matter what you ask him, he never makes you feel foolish, like you should already know the answer. Boys at the academy talk about him with awe, and now I know why. I can't believe I'm going to study under him. There were only a few in my class who were selected for the institute, and I'm one of them."

Sarah studied her brother as he spoke. Except for the mustache, he resembled their father at around the same age. She knew because her parents' wedding photo was on the table beside her bed, and she looked at it almost daily.

Tom gestured with his hands as he shared more stories. They would soon be the hands of a doctor. Hands that would be used to soothe and heal. Oh, how proud their parents would be of the man Tom had become.

Would they be equally proud of her? Or would she be a disappointment to them? Her schooling had ended when she was sixteen. She'd never traveled farther than Boise City, never seen an ocean, never been to any of the large cities in the east nor to any foreign country. All she knew of the world was what she'd read in books. She was nearly twenty-two and unmarried while most of her friends had husbands and families of their own.

Of course, she could have been married long before this. Warren West had first proposed to her when she was sixteen. She'd turned him down because she wanted to travel the world, to see places far beyond this valley. She'd wanted something...more. In addition, the man she'd imagined marrying had been so different from Warren. A handsome nobleman who rode up on a magnificent horse or perhaps a brooding hero like Mr. Rochester or a proud one like Mr. Darcy. Never once had she imagined Warren West.

Undaunted, he'd proposed again when Sarah turned seventeen. Another refusal. That year, she'd thought she might study medicine, like her brother. She could be a nurse and work with Tom. That would be her ticket to new adventures.

When Warren asked her again on her eighteenth birthday, she'd told him maybe. She knew by then she didn't want to be a nurse, and the longed-for travel was beyond her reach. As for her romantic fantasies, she'd decided they were foolish. She would never meet an English lord or a European count or a Mr. Rochester or a Mr. Darcy.

Still, she hadn't accepted that proposal. Or the one after that.

"Marry Warren," her grandmother had urged. *"He's a good man. He'll provide well for you. Don't waste your life wishing for things you cannot have."*

And so, when Warren proposed once again on Sarah's twenty-first birthday, she agreed to marry him in one year. Her grandmother had passed away by then, but at least Sarah knew the decision would have made Grandma happy.

But am I happy?

"What do you think, Sarah?"

Her brother's question brought her attention abruptly to the present. "I'm sorry. What did you—"

"Daydreaming, sis?" He glanced at their grandfather. "Remember when we used to go fishing at your favorite spot on the river and she'd sit on those rocks and stare off into space, dreaming about the Eiffel Tower and Buckingham

Palace and pretending she was royalty or something? She had that same look on her face just now."

"I remember." Grandpa turned a fond gaze on her. "And I wish I could've made all those dreams come true for her."

She felt a tightness in her chest. Whatever would she do if he were to die? He'd been the rock she depended on all her life. Shaking off the melancholy thought, she said, "If they'd come true, you would have to call me Lady Sarah whenever you visited me in the castle."

Tom hopped to his feet, swept off an imaginary hat, and executed an elaborate bow. "Lady Sarah, how kind of you to allow your lowly kinfolk to join you for lunch in your beautiful castle."

"Do sit down, my good fellow." She stuck her nose in the air and sent him a censuring glance. "The servants shall clear the table soon, and you're liable to trip them."

Both men laughed.

She grinned, concerns for her grandfather—and her approaching wedding day—forgotten.

"I'll help you clear." Tom picked up a few dirty dishes. "And I promise not to trip any of the servants."

She pushed away the niggling doubts about her bridegroom and led the way into the kitchen.

THREE

As evening crept over the valley, Jeremiah shoved more wood into the stove, thankful for the plentiful supply he'd found stacked against the side of the house. There might even be enough to see him through the winter. But firewood wasn't his most pressing problem. He could always go into the forest and cut more wood if necessary. No, the real problem was money.

He'd told Warren he would pay him half the value of the farm. He'd felt guilty. That's why he'd made the offer. Guilt. Needing to right a wrong. A familiar feeling. But he did owe it to his brother. The son who'd stayed behind. The son who'd done what was expected. Unlike Jeremiah.

Why had their dad left the farm to him? He couldn't figure it out. Sure, he was the oldest of the two West boys, but that wasn't much of a reason. Not after the way they'd parted. Even now, he could hear the final words they'd hurled at each other.

"You're a fool, Jeremiah. You'll never amount to anything."

"You're wrong."

"You can't provide for a wife. You'll both die of starvation. See if you won't. You can't take care of yourself, let alone a woman."

"I love Marta. I'm going to marry her."

"Not and live under my roof."

"That's fine with me. Good riddance to your roof."

Turning from the stove, he glanced around the main room. It seemed as if, any moment, his dad might walk through the door. The living area looked exactly the same as it had all those years ago. Not that he should be surprised. Ted West had been a man of habit and routine. He suspected Warren was much the same.

Jeremiah sank onto a chair and stared at the flickering orange flames inside the black belly of the stove. He supposed the familiarity was one reason he'd come back. He'd wanted to make peace with his past—and with himself. If he could. Outside, the wind whistled through the trees, a lonely wail in the darkness of a winter's night.

He closed his eyes, listening to the crackle in the stove and the wail beyond the walls, contrasting sounds, one friendly, one not so. He listened and felt the isolation surround him.

"Well, I'm back. Now what?"

ALL THROUGH SUPPER THAT EVENING, SARAH HAD THE FEELING something troubled Warren. She didn't know what it might be, and he didn't let on. That was like Warren. He kept his thoughts to himself. "Don't worry your pretty little head," he often said to her when she asked what he was thinking.

What on earth would they talk about after they got married?

She looked at her fiancé across the table. What was she

supposed to feel about their upcoming wedding? Excitement? Anticipation? Joy? Because she felt none of those things. Were those feelings only the stuff of novels?

That must be it. Maybe she wanted emotions that weren't realistic. Everyone told her how lucky she was. Warren was liked throughout Boulder Creek. Other girls would have gladly married him if he hadn't been set on marrying her. She should be thankful he cared for her.

Grandma had said marriage was like being wrapped in a comfortable old quilt. There was nothing exciting about an old quilt. She was foolish to long to feel...more.

Supper over, Sarah cleared the table and washed the dishes while the men retired to her grandfather's study for a smoke and a glass of whiskey. By the time she'd dried and put away the last plate, the three of them had returned to the parlor.

Warren sat beside her on the upholstered sofa her grandmother had ordered from the Montgomery Ward catalogue a few years before she passed. He took hold of Sarah's hand and squeezed her fingers. "I've got some news to share." He waited until he had everyone's attention. "My brother has returned."

Grandpa's eyebrows rose. "Jeremiah's in Boulder Creek?"

"Yes. He's staying at the farm."

"Well, I'll be." Grandpa shook his head. "I never expected him to come back."

"Anybody care to fill me in?" Tom looked at Warren. "I didn't even know you *had* a brother."

Sarah wasn't like Tom. She'd known about Jeremiah. Perhaps she'd met him when she was a child. But Warren never talked about his brother, and something in his manner had kept her from asking questions.

Grandpa looked at the ceiling, as if that would help him recall facts. "Let's see. Jeremiah must've been about seventeen or eighteen when he and Marta Parkerson ran off together. When was that?" He was silent for several moments. "About 'eighty-five, I reckon. It was spring, as I recall. Time for planting. Marta was barely sixteen. Darn fool youngsters, the both of them." He looked at Tom. "Guess you would've been about four when they ran off."

Sarah's eyes widened. "They eloped?" She'd never heard that part of the story. How romantic. Two young people so much in love they would defy the world to be together.

Grandpa nodded. "Caused a ruckus around these parts. Mrs. Parkerson took it real hard, having her only child run off like that, and she wasn't ever the same until the day she died." He frowned. "We heard Marta died in the influenza pandemic of 1889. The baby she carried was born and died with her."

"How terrible for Jeremiah." Sarah looked at Warren. "Has he come back to stay?"

"He plans to work the farm. He says he'll buy out my share."

"But that's wonderful, Warren. Your brother is home. We must do something to make him feel welcome."

His hand tightened on hers. "It's not wonderful. Now I can't sell the farm, and I counted on that money to pay for the wedding trip."

She felt a sting of disappointment. No trip to New York and Philadelphia. She would never see The Assembly, not even from the outside. But that was selfish! Jeremiah had lost his wife and newborn child. Now he'd come home after all these years. He should be welcomed, not begrudged the family farm.

"We'll take our trip another time," she said with determined cheerfulness. "Having your brother home again is much more important."

Warren turned a dark look in her direction. "I want you to stay away from him."

"But—"

"He'll only cause trouble. He's always caused trouble. Stay away from him, Sarah. I mean it."

FOUR

J eremiah returned to the mercantile the next day with a list of supplies he needed. As George Blake filled the order, Jeremiah said, "By chance would you know of any job openings?"

George paused to look at him. "I thought you meant to work your dad's farm."

"I do. But spring is a ways off, and I could use some wages now."

"Sawmill doesn't need anybody. You might find work at the Rocking D, although most of Will's men have been with him for years." His eyes narrowed. "You know, the sheriff is in need of a deputy. Last one left Boulder Creek in the spring and nobody's replaced him. Don't know why Sheriff McNeal has gone without the help so long."

"McNeal is still the sheriff? *Hank* McNeal?"

George nodded. "Yes, and he's no spring chicken."

"No, he wouldn't be." Jeremiah remembered the man from his boyhood scrapes with the law. Nothing serious. But he used to make his share of mischief around Boulder Creek. Sheriff

McNeal had been a stern but fair man and had shown Jeremiah plenty of grace. More than his own father had.

"With your experience in the army and the war and this being your hometown and all, you could be the right man for the job."

A sheriff's deputy? He'd never thought about doing that kind of work.

"Why don't you go talk to McNeal while we finish putting together your order?"

What would Warren think if Jeremiah became the town's deputy? His gut told him his brother wouldn't like it. Maybe because he hoped Jeremiah would tire of farming and leave Boulder Creek again. Sooner rather than later.

"Pay oughta be decent enough," George added.

"I'll talk to him." What else could he do? He needed the money to pay Warren for his share of the land. If the deputy position was his only choice for a job, then he'd better try to get it.

"You remember where the McNeal house is? That's where you'll probably find him at this time of day."

"I remember. Big house. It had blue shutters."

"Still does. Used to sit all alone, too, but it's got a street running in front of it now. North Street. Got neighbors on both side of it and across the street too. You'll see."

Jeremiah glanced out the window. "I never expected things to change this much while I was away."

"People we don't see anymore never age from the way we last saw them. Guess it's the same with a town. Stays the same in our memories, I reckon."

"I reckon," Jeremiah echoed softly, thoughts drifting.

He remembered Marta when he'd asked her to marry him. Slender as a reed. Round dark eyes. Her hair a reddish brown, thick and curly. She hadn't been strong, physically, but she'd had the will of a lion. She'd made him feel like a good man, not the troublesome boy others thought him. If he hadn't taken her away, maybe she'd still be alive. That was something he had to live with. He couldn't change the past, but his decisions today could change his future. That's what a man he served with in the army had told him. Make better decisions today so you make tomorrow better too.

"I'll go see the sheriff." He stepped back from the counter. "I'll return for the supplies in a bit."

From her second-story bedroom window, Sarah stared across North Street at the idle waterwheel attached to the side of Boulder Creek Lumber. In the spring, summer, and early fall, the wheel turned rapidly, forced into action by the cold waters of Pony Creek, but in the dead of winter, when the water in the creek was low—or frozen as it was now—the wheel stood silent and still. Rather like the McNeal house at the moment.

Tom and Grandpa had gone to visit with Doc Varney, and their absence made Sarah realize how much more alive their home had felt since Tom's return. How she would miss him when he left to begin his medical training.

She sighed as she sat on the window seat, tucking her legs beneath her skirt and drawing her knees toward her chest. Once comfortable, she reached for the well-read issue of the *Ladies' Home Journal* that lay nearby. The magazine fell open to an illustration of dancers swirling about a chandelier-lit ballroom. She knew most of the words by heart, but she read them anyway.

During just one hundred and fifty years the entrance into "society" in Philadelphia has been through the doorway of "The Assembly." The managers of the functions of that annual court of honor have been foremost in regulating the social sovereignty of the city. Nowhere else in the United States is there a dynasty which has held longer or more nearly uninterrupted sway.

As she had countless times before, Sarah imagined what it would be like to walk through those doors on the arm of a dashing escort, her gown made of satin and lace and a tiara in her hair. Tall and incredibly handsome, her escort would wear a black dress suit. Heads would turn, and people would whisper, wondering who she was, who he was, who they were.

Indeed, the City Dancing Assembly of Philadelphia was in existence before the aristocracy of Charleston had begun their Cæcilia, and even before the far-famed Almack's was founded as the seventh heaven of the fashionable set in London.

The orchestra would play for hours and hours, and Sarah would dance and dance and dance. She would laugh softly and politely at her escort's jokes, but she would not allow him to presume she felt more for him than was proper. She would—

A loud rapping at the front door disturbed her daydreams. A rush of guilt followed. She should daydream about Warren, but try as she might, she'd never been able to imagine him waltzing with her. Warren was so...so...Warren.

The caller knocked again.

With a sigh, she set aside the magazine and hurried from her room. While she was still on the stairs, the visitor knocked a third time.

"Just a moment," she called, quickening her steps.

She pulled open the door, expecting to find a familiar face, but instead there stood a stranger—a very tall, very handsome stranger. A stranger who could have been the mysterious escort of her daydreams had he worn an evening suit and silk hat.

"Excuse me." He touched the broad brim of his black cavalry hat with two fingers. "I'm looking for Sheriff McNeal. I thought this was his house."

His voice had a deep, pleasant resonance that caused something to curl inside her. Did she hear the stirring notes of *The Blue Danube* playing in the background?

One dark eyebrow arched as the stranger looked down at her. "I expected to remember which house it was, but everything's changed. If you could tell me where he lives—"

"I'm sorry." She felt embarrassment rising in her cheeks. He must think her stupid, the way she'd stared at him. "This *is* Sheriff McNeal's home, but he isn't here at the moment."

"I checked at the jail. No one was there."

"No, he went with my brother to see someone. I'm his granddaughter, Sarah McNeal. Perhaps I can help you."

He shook his head. "No, it's the sheriff I need to see. Would you tell him Jeremiah West was by and wants to talk to him?"

"Jeremiah?"

This was Warren's brother? But they didn't look anything alike. Jeremiah's hair was dark, almost black, and his eyes were the color of coal mixed with soot. His features were chiseled, masculine, powerful. The two men were close to the same height, but something about Jeremiah made him seem taller.

Realizing she was staring again, she fought back another blush. "Do come in." She opened the door wider. "Please. Grandpa won't be much longer. He and my brother should be back soon."

"Well, I—"

"You've come all this way from the farm, and it's too cold to wait outside."

He hesitated a moment longer before removing his hat and stepping through the open doorway. "This is kind of you, Miss McNeal."

"Please, call me Sarah. Miss McNeal sounds so formal." She almost added that he would soon be her brother-in-law, but the words caught in her throat. "Come into the parlor and warm yourself by the fire. I'll get you some coffee."

"Don't go to any trouble."

"It's no trouble. The coffee's made."

She left him in the parlor and hurried into the kitchen. A hundred questions raced through her head as she snatched two cups from the cupboard and filled them with the dark brew. In no time at all, she carried a tray to the parlor.

Jeremiah waited near the window, hat in hand, while she set the tray on a low table. After she'd taken her place on the sofa, he moved to the chair opposite her.

"Do you take cream or sugar, Jeremiah?"

"No. Just black, thanks."

She held out the china cup and saucer toward him. When he reached for them, their fingers touched. Sarah felt that odd curling sensation in her stomach again. Quickly, she withdrew her hand, fighting to restore order within.

"Tom, my brother, arrived home yesterday." She lifted her own cup. "You must have been on the same train, and we didn't know it." She remembered the man, standing in the shadows of the passenger car, watching her. It could have been

Jeremiah. Her heart skipped at the realization. "Isn't that a strange coincidence, Mr. West?"

"Strange," he said softly.

The word reverberated in her chest, and the parlor walls seemed to grow closer, the room becoming small and intimate.

"Miss McNeal—"

"Sarah, please. And since we are to be family soon, may I call you Jeremiah?"

"What?"

"You'd rather I didn't use your given name?"

"I don't understand. What do you mean, we're to be family?"

"But surely Warren told you."

His dark brows drew together.

"I thought you knew. Warren and I are engaged to be married."

FIVE

S he was exquisitely beautiful, his brother's intended, and there was an innocence in her sky blue eyes that made Jeremiah feel old and jaded. He remembered the way she'd welcomed that young man—her brother, she'd said—at the train station. He remembered the look of utter joy and the warm glow her happiness had cast all around her.

Warren was a lucky man.

Jeremiah cleared his throat. "Congratulations, Miss McNeal. I hope you and my brother will have a long and happy marriage."

"Please, you must call me Sarah." The smile vanished from her mouth. "I'm very sorry for your loss. I...I remember Marta a little. She was a sweet girl."

"Yes, she was." He looked down into the cup in his hand. He didn't want to be rude, but neither did he want to talk about his deceased wife. Nine years hadn't made it easier to remember the way he'd lost her. So young. If he'd been a better provider, if he'd known what to do when she'd started to take ill, if he'd sent for the doctor sooner—

The front door opened, and cold air swept into the parlor. Jeremiah rose from his chair, glad for the interruption. Moments later, Hank McNeal paused in the entry to the living room, his gaze moving from Sarah to Jeremiah. He was no longer the same physically threatening authority figure, but his eyes were as steely as ever and they assessed Jeremiah with a quick but thorough look.

"Welcome back," Hank said at last. He stepped forward and offered his hand.

"Thank you, sir."

"Jeremiah's been waiting to speak to you, Grandpa," Sarah interjected.

"Have you now? Well, that's fine. Just fine." Hank stepped back and turned toward the younger man waiting behind him. "I don't suppose you remember my grandson. He was mighty young when you left town. Tom, this is Jeremiah West."

Like his grandfather, Tom stepped forward and shook Jeremiah's hand. The young man was a slightly darker, more masculine version of Sarah. His blue eyes revealed quick intelligence, and his smile was warm and friendly. "Pleased to meet you, Mr. West."

"The same." He returned his gaze to Hank. "I wonder if I might have a word with you, sir. George Blake told me the town's looking for a deputy. I'm interested in the job."

"Is that right? Well, come with me to my study." The sheriff motioned with his head, then led the way.

Jeremiah gave a nod to Sarah and Tom before following the older man.

Hank's study was a small, cluttered room at the back of the house, filled with an oak desk and lined with bookshelves. The room smelled of leather and pipe smoke. A man's domain.

"Have a seat." Hank motioned to a chair. Then he walked

slowly around to the one behind the desk. "So, you're interested in being the deputy?"

"Yes, sir. Yes, I am."

"You never struck me as the deputy sort, Jeremiah. If memory serves, you caused more trouble than you ever stopped." The words were softened by an amused glint in his eyes.

"Yeah, I guess I did. I'll be honest with you, sir. I've never been a deputy. Never even thought it a possibility. But I've been a soldier. I know how to follow orders."

"Tell me what other experience you've got."

He drew in a deep breath. "I've done a lot of things since I left Boulder Creek. Farmed a little place back in Ohio for a few years. After Marta...after she died, I didn't care to stay on there so I moved around. Did some mining, tended bar in a saloon, worked cattle on a ranch in Montana for a while. Spent a year with the railroad, laying track and blasting through rock. A few years back, I went to New York and worked in a factory, assembling motors. After that, I joined the army. It was when I was in Cuba that I realized it was time for me to return to Boulder Creek." He paused a moment, then shook his head. "I'm not sure what kind of a deputy I'd be. But I need the job, and I'll do the best I can."

The sheriff nodded, as if digesting what Jeremiah had told him. Finally, he asked, "Ever been in trouble with the law? Real trouble, I mean. Not the set-downs I gave you when you were a boy."

"No, sir."

"I expect you know plenty about using a gun after being in the army."

A muscle in Jeremiah's jaw flinched. "Yes."

"I heard you were wounded. Your leg bother you any?"

He'd forgotten how fast news traveled in this town. He guessed everyone knew he was back, along with everything else he'd told Leslie Blake yesterday. "My leg's sound. I've got a bit of a limp, but it doesn't hamper my ability to get around. I can run and I can ride a horse."

Hank glanced out the window. "Boulder Creek's a quiet town, for the most part. We had a bit of trouble in the years you were away but mostly, being the deputy here means letting somebody sleep off a bit too much whiskey in the jail, breaking up a fight at the saloon now and then, collecting taxes that aren't paid on time, issuing licenses, occasionally looking for rustlers, that sort of thing." His gaze returned to meet Jeremiah's. "Not very exciting work for someone who's traveled the country like you have."

"I'm not looking for excitement, sir. I'm looking to settle down, to put down roots of my own."

Hank leaned against the back of his chair. "Care to tell me what you did in the war?"

Memories flooded his mind. The boredom. The heat. The flies. The stench. The sickness. The blood. The young boys, their bodies bloating, lying open-eyed on the battlefield. He drew a breath and answered, "I did whatever I was told to do by my superior officers."

"And you plan to stay in Boulder Creek?"

"Yes, sir. Like I said, I'm ready to put down roots. The farm is mine. I plan to work it."

For a second time, the sheriff turned his gaze out the window. Jeremiah didn't know what the older man saw.

After a lengthy silence, Hank said, "I got to know your pa pretty well over the years. Ted was a decent man. I know he could be strict with you boys. Hard at times. Father raising his sons alone has to be, I reckon. But he was proud of you both. Mighty proud."

The last comment surprised Jeremiah. He couldn't remember his dad being proud of him for anything. He could only remember how often he'd been told what a disappointment he was, how he'd never amount to much.

"He missed you after you left." Hank looked at him again. "He'd be glad to know you've come home. And I reckon you'll make a good deputy." He stood and held out his hand. "You've got the job if you want it. You think on it and let me know after church on Sunday. And plan to have dinner with us. Don't bother to say no. We'll be expecting you."

———

SARAH HEARD THE MEN'S VOICES IN THE HALL AND STOOD. A MOMENT later, she heard her grandfather bid Jeremiah a good day, followed by the sound of the closing door. Disappointment sluiced through her. She'd wanted a chance to talk to Jeremiah again. She'd wanted to get to know him better. To really know him. After all, he would soon be a brother to her.

Her conscience twinged. Was that the *real* reason she wanted to know him? Something in her heart said otherwise.

Grandpa entered the parlor. "Nice young man."

"Did he tell you where he's been all these years?" Sarah asked.

Grandpa shook his head. "A little." He gave her a searching look as he settled onto his favorite chair near the fire. "Man's got a right to his privacy."

Tom asked, "Are you giving him the job as your deputy?"

"More'n likely. I told him to think about it and to let me know on Sunday. He'll be with us for dinner."

A shiver passed through Sarah.

"What will Warren have to say about that?" Tom looked between Grandpa and Sarah. "After what he said yesterday, I don't imagine he'll be keen on the idea of Jeremiah getting the job *or* coming to dinner."

Sarah tilted her chin. "I'll speak to Warren. They're brothers. They should make peace with each other."

"You may not be able to fix the trouble between them, sis. You said yourself you don't know what went wrong between them. Besides, Jeremiah was gone a long time. They're almost strangers."

"You were gone a long time, too."

Tom laughed softly. "Not fourteen years. People change in that amount of time. You'd better leave it up to Warren and Jeremiah to work things out."

Sarah rose and carried the tray to the kitchen. "It won't hurt for me to try to help."

"Be careful," Tom called after her. "That's all I'm saying."

Standing at the sink, Sarah stared out the window, looking down North Street. It took a moment to realize she'd hoped for a glimpse of Jeremiah West, but he was nowhere in sight.

As Jeremiah guided the rented horse and sleigh down the street, he heard the shouts of the school children as they played a game of tag in the schoolyard. At the corner, he paused for a moment to watch them, and his thoughts drifted through the years to his own boyhood.

He remembered when that schoolhouse had been built. Adelaide Danson had been the schoolteacher then. There'd been plenty of excitement over the books and desks and chalkboards, all of them as brand new as the building itself. He recalled the smell of wet wool from coats and scarves and mittens hanging on hooks on the back wall and the way the single room had felt in winter—either too hot or too cold, depending on how far away a desk was from the fat black stove in the corner.

Good memories. A nice change.

With a shake of his head, he turned the horse in the direction of the farm. The runners on the wagon bed slid across the hard-packed snow with a steady *whoosh*. As the sleigh crossed the bridge over Pony Creek, Jeremiah glanced to his right at the lumber mill and thought of his dad.

Ted West had gone to work at the mill soon after he and his sons settled in the valley. He'd worked the land on the farm after his regular mill shift, making for long days. Yet Jeremiah couldn't recall hearing his dad complain.

A longing rose unexpectedly in his chest. He wished he could talk to his dad. He wished he could say he was sorry. He'd like to say he regretted all the things he'd done that had caused his dad grief. His quick temper. His impatience. His running away. And especially how sorry he was about the money he'd taken from his dad's dresser drawer. But it was too late for sorries to matter. Too late to make amends, no matter how much he wished he could do so.

"If wishes were horses, beggars would ride." That's what his dad used to say.

All too true.

"Get up there." He slapped the reins against the horse's rump, hoping he could outrun his troubling thoughts.

As if to prove he hadn't mastered the ability to take every thought captive, Sarah McNeal's image replaced that of his father. He remembered the kindness in her eyes. He pictured her lovely face with its milky complexion and tiny, turned-up nose and heart-shaped mouth, soft and pink. He recalled the smooth sweep of her hair, the golden brown tresses dressed high and loosely brushed back from her forehead.

And finally—perhaps too late—he remembered that she

was engaged to marry his brother. If he sought peace in Boulder Creek, he'd best keep himself and his thoughts clear of Miss Sarah McNeal.

CHAPTER
SIX

J eremiah dropped hay into the feed trough for the gelding. Tomorrow, he would return the rented rig and horse to the livery and buy a mount of his own. He would need a saddle horse to get back and forth to town once he started working as the deputy. And, when the time came, he would buy a plow horse too.

He turned from the stall, his gaze sweeping the barn's interior. Light from the lantern didn't reach far, but he already knew the work that awaited him. Winter was a good time to get things back in order. The harness and plow both needed repairs, and he would have to buy some tools as well. He supposed Warren had taken their father's tools when he moved into town. Part of him wanted to resent that—the farm had been left to Jeremiah, not Warren, which meant the tools were his. Another part of him understood Warren's actions.

How can I make things right between us?

With a shake of his head, he took the lantern from the hook and headed outside. A bitter wind met him, and he leaned his head and shoulders into it as he strode to the house.

Inside, he shrugged out of his coat and hung it on a hook near the door, thankful he'd tended to the fire before feeding the horse. He crossed to the stove and stared at the dancing flames in its belly. The crackle of the fire was all that broke the silence inside the house. Jeremiah didn't usually mind quiet and solitude, but tonight it reminded him how alone he was.

He sank onto the nearby chair, memories intruding on the silence.

Those few short years with Marta by his side had been the best and the worst. The best because she'd loved him and been his helpmeet, the way the Good Book said it was meant to be between a husband and wife. The worst because he hadn't been able to do for her all that he'd promised when they'd run off together, and because of it, she'd died. She and their newborn son.

Their deaths had ripped his heart clear out of his chest. He'd wanted to die for a long time, but God hadn't seen fit to take him, not even when he'd been reckless with his life. Not even in the bloody, terrible war in Cuba with all the disease and shooting that had surrounded him.

He closed his eyes.

Nine years had come and gone since Marta's death. The piercing pain had stopped after a few years, but the yearning for what he'd lost came back to haunt him sometimes. Like tonight, with the silence in this house.

Marta wouldn't want him to be alone. She'd told him so. But he didn't know how to change that. It wouldn't be by taking himself another wife. He'd lost one. He wasn't about to lose another. He didn't have the ability to love a woman anymore. His heart was too damaged. It wasn't his to give.

Maybe when he went into town tomorrow he'd see about a dog. There must be somebody in Boulder Creek or one of the surrounding farms and ranches who had a litter of pups they wanted to be rid of. A dog would fill the empty space and chase away the silence.

SARAH LIFTED THE CURTAINS AND STARED OUT AT THE MOONLIT street. "Do you suppose the baby's arrived by now, Grandpa?"

"Could be. Never know about these things. Some women have a difficult time. Others not so much. There's just no telling."

"I wish I could have gone with Tom and the doctor to the James's ranch."

"Childbirthing's no place for an unmarried girl."

Sarah knew more about childbirth—and conception— than her grandfather would like. She knew because she'd stolen a look at some of the medical books her brother had brought home from Doc Varney's about four years ago. The information in those books had shocked her and, at the same time, made her glad she was no longer kept in ignorance.

"Your mother had long labors with both you and Tom, but she said it was worth it, bringing new life into the world."

Sarah turned from the window. "Tell me something about her. Something you haven't told me before."

Grandpa smiled. "A lot like you, princess. She made your pa mighty happy, and your grandma said God gave her another daughter to love when Thomas senior married Maria. It was true. It surely was."

It wasn't a new story he told her, but she treasured the words all the same as she knelt on the rug beside her grandfather's chair and leaned her arms on his thigh.

Grandpa stroked her hair. "Your pa built this house when he and Maria first came to Boulder Creek. They wanted a house full of children. Each time your ma lost a baby, it near broke her heart. And then you came along." He lightly pinched the tip of her nose. "You wrapped us all around your little finger from the very start."

Sarah laughed softly, but she knew it was true, at least about her grandparents. Doris McNeal, the grandmother who'd raised Sarah and Tom, had seldom been able to say no, no matter what mischief the two of them got into. And there'd been plenty of mischief, at least where Tom was concerned. He'd been a grand one for thinking up ways to make trouble.

"Tom's going to make a wonderful doctor, isn't he?"

Grandpa didn't seem the least bit surprised by the turn her thoughts had taken. "Yep, he is."

Sarah closed her eyes, listening to the crackling fire. Such a warm and friendly sound. It spoke of home and family.

Cold air *whooshed* into the room from the entry hall. "He's back!" She jumped to her feet even as she heard the door close.

Tom entered the parlor, his cheeks red from the cold, his eyes shining with excitement. "It's a healthy baby boy."

"And Skylark?" Sarah asked.

"She's fine. Mr. James, too." He pulled off his coat and hat, then disappeared into the entry to hang up the winter garments. When he returned, he asked, "Any coffee made? I'm frozen clear through."

"Yes, I thought you might want some. I'll get it for you." She headed toward the kitchen, pausing to give her brother a quick kiss on the cheek. "Come with me. I want to hear more."

Tom glanced at their grandfather.

"Go on with your sister. I'm ready to turn in for the night. We can talk again in the morning."

Sarah filled two cups with coffee and set one on the table in front of Tom. She took the chair across from him, watching him fold his hands around the hot cup, absorbing its warmth.

"Now tell me everything you learned tonight."

"I don't think that's a subject I should discuss with an unmarried female."

"You sound just like Grandpa." She kicked him under the table.

"Ouch!" He leaned down to grab his shin.

"I'll be a married woman soon enough. And besides, I know more than you think I do."

"Only about ballrooms and the peerage of England," he muttered, then grinned at her as he leaned forward, his arms braced on the table. "It was the most amazing experience I've had in my whole life, Sarah. Doc Varney let me watch the delivery. I was right there at his side. As if he already thinks of me as a fellow doctor. Yale...I mean, Mr. James, he was outside, pacing up and down, but I was in the room with the doc. And Sarah, it was amazing. It's like a miracle, seeing a baby born." Emotion filled his voice.

In response, tears sprang to her eyes. "I'm proud of you, Tom. You're going to make such a wonderful doctor."

The corners of his mouth tipped. "I think tonight I might really believe that could be true."

SEVEN

As if he'd never missed a Sunday in Boulder Creek, Jeremiah went to the same pew at the back of the church where he used to sit beside his father and brother.

In Ohio, he and Marta had been faithful church-goers, but after her death, things had changed for him. When he first began wandering, it had been because there were no churches nearby, but later it was because he'd found it easier to pray when he was by himself. And he'd done plenty of talking to God through the years.

But how much listening have I done?

As the question whispered in his mind, his gaze swept over the pews. Perhaps being back in Boulder Creek would improve his ability to hear from the good Lord.

Some in the church were strangers to Jeremiah, but there were familiar faces as well. A few had been students with him at the Boulder Creek school. Now those former schoolmates had families of their own. Others had grown old, and some were noticeably absent.

He recognized pretty Rosalie Tomkin. Except, according to

Leslie Blake, she was Rosalie Randolph now, wife to Michael Randolph, the town's mayor as well as owner of the Randolph Hotel. Between her and the man he assumed was Michael sat two young children, a boy and a girl.

Old Doc Varney sat across the aisle from the Randolphs. The doctor had grown somewhat heavier over the years, but he looked as hale and alert as ever. A woman with gray hair tucked beneath a velvet hat sat close by the older man's side. Did Doc have a wife now? It would seem so.

George and Leslie Blake sat in front of Doc Varney, joined by Leslie's sister, Annalee, her husband, and their three children, the youngest one he supposed no more than a year old.

Jeremiah's gaze stopped wandering when he spotted Sarah McNeal, seated between her brother and grandfather. A more attractive vision, he couldn't remember seeing, in church or out. Almost angelic. She wore a gown of blue, the same sky-blue shade as her eyes. A matching felt hat perched atop her hair at a jaunty angle.

Pastor Jacobs—Jeremiah had met the man the previous day—stepped to the pulpit and motioned with his hands for the congregation to rise. "Let us sing, 'A Mighty Fortress is Our God.'"

Jeremiah's gaze lingered a short while longer on the woman in blue, then he forced himself to focus on the words of the hymn. A better choice for his soul...and his relationship with his brother.

IN HIS REED-THIN VOICE, REVEREND JACOBS SAID, "ROMANS, THE twelfth chapter, tells us this: 'If it be possible, as much as lieth in you, live peaceably with all men.'" His gaze moved around the sanctuary.

Sarah felt her cheeks grow hot. Did the pastor know about the disagreement she'd had with Warren that very same morning—the disagreement that had sent her intended back to his living quarters above the workshop instead of coming to church with her? The unspoken question caused the words they'd exchanged on her doorstep to replay in her mind.

"I told you to keep away from him, Sarah."

"Grandpa invited him to eat with us. I couldn't uninvite him."

"Well, don't expect me to sit down to eat with Jeremiah at the table."

"Warren, he's your brother. Your only living relative. Shouldn't you try to get along? You're being unreasonable."

"I'm telling you. He will not be welcome in our home after we're married. Understand me?"

She closed her eyes, a weight pressing on her chest.

After we're married.

The words sent a chill through her. Was it the thought of marriage itself that disturbed her or was it the dictatorial way Warren had spoken to her? Would she have no say in who could be a guest in their home?

Live peaceably with all men. Wasn't that what Reverend Jacobs just said? Warren should have been in church to hear that bit of the sermon. He should know God expected him to make peace with his brother.

She felt Grandpa and Tom stir and rise on either side of her, and she opened her eyes and joined them for the closing hymn. As she sang, her gaze traveled across the aisle to where Jeremiah stood. His voice carried to her, strong and deep, and something quite different from a chill vibrated through her at the sound. The words of the hymn caught in her throat as she snapped her eyes forward once more.

This wouldn't do. Whatever these strange feelings were, they wouldn't do at all.

As soon as the service was over, Sarah hurried outside, welcoming the brisk temperature. The skies were leaden, and the air smelled of snow.

"Is something wrong, Sarah?"

She faced Grandpa. "No. But I need to hurry home to see to our Sunday dinner." She glanced behind him. "Where's Tom?"

"Someone over at the hotel is sick, and they sent for the doctor. Tom went along to observe." He turned toward the church doors. "But here's Jeremiah and Mrs. Varney. We can go on home. Doc and Tom will join us as soon as they can."

As Jeremiah approached, he gave Sarah a brief smile before returning his attention to the doctor's wife whose hand had settled in the crook of his arm. Sarah wished she could trade places with the woman.

Absurd notion.

"Let's get on home," Grandpa said again. "The pastor's sermon worked up a hunger in me."

She forced a smile. "Good idea. It's growing colder by the minute." She took her grandfather's arm.

As soon as they were in the house and had shed their coats, Sarah and Betsy Varney went into the kitchen. The roast that had been put into the oven before the family left for church was done to perfection, and with two women working together, the rest of the meal was ready in short order. They were setting the food on the table when Doc and Tom entered the house, their hats and coats dusted slightly with snow.

"Your timing is perfect," Grandpa said, standing behind the chair at the head of the table.

Sarah gave her brother's arm a light punch. "Of course it is. Tom always knows when food's ready."

Tom laughed. "Guilty." He moved to the chair at the foot of the table.

Within moments, the rest of the party had found places around the large table.

"It's kind of you to include me." Jeremiah settled onto the chair to her grandfather's right, directly opposite Sarah.

"Glad you could join us," Grandpa answered. "We hope it'll be the first of many such occasions."

Grandpa might hope that, but Sarah knew her future husband didn't feel the same way.

As if hearing her thought, Jeremiah looked at her. "Warren isn't coming?"

"No." She glanced from him to her grandfather and back again. "No, he...he couldn't be here today."

Something flickered in Jeremiah's eyes, and she knew he'd guessed that he was the reason for his brother's absence.

"Well," Grandpa said, "let's bless the food and eat before it gets cold." He bowed his head, and everyone followed suit.

As soon as the brief prayer ended, they passed platters and bowls around the table. Laughter and chatter filled the room. The wintry day outside was forgotten amidst the warmth of the gathering of family and friends.

Sarah noticed the way Jeremiah listened to others, soaking in the conversation like the land soaked in rain after a drought. Occasionally a smile tipped the corners of his mouth, and when that happened, something squeezed inside her chest. There was a sorrow within him that he tried to hide, but also strength and resilience. Her heart told her that he was a good man who only wanted to belong once again.

A knock sounded at the front door. Someone disturbing the McNeal's Sunday dinner usually meant trouble of one kind or another. They might want the sheriff or, since Doc was their guest today, they might need the doctor.

Tom rose. "I'll see who it is." He disappeared from the

dining room, returning a short while later with Warren following behind.

"Sorry I'm late," Warren said.

"There's plenty of food left." Grandpa motioned toward a chair against the wall. "Pull that up and join us. Doc and Tom'll make room for you."

Warren's gaze met with Sarah's. Then he looked at Jeremiah, his countenance darkening. Finally, he did as suggested, sliding the chair into place between Tom and Doc.

Sarah knew what her grandfather had done. By placing Warren and Jeremiah on the same side of the long table, with Doc in between them, they wouldn't have to look at each other. Still, some of the pleasant mood had drained from the room with Warren's arrival.

Close to an hour later, while Betsy helped Sarah with the dishes, Jeremiah and Grandpa went into the study, and Warren, Tom, and Doc settled in the parlor.

"What's wrong with Warren?" Betsy asked in a hushed voice.

Sarah shook her head, more because she didn't want to answer than because she didn't understand. Warren was angry and bitter about the farm, but it wasn't Jeremiah's fault. Anybody with a lick of sense would know that.

The door to Grandpa's study opened just as Sarah and Betsy joined the others in the parlor. Grandpa shook Jeremiah's hand and Sarah heard him say, "I'll see you first thing in the morning."

"Yes, sir. You will."

Jeremiah turned his gaze on everyone in the parlor. "I need to get back to the farm. Glad we could sit down to Sunday dinner together." He looked at Sarah. "I haven't enjoyed a meal this much in a long time, Miss McNeal. Thank you."

"You're welcome, Jeremiah."

She caught Warren's displeasure at her use of his brother's given name. She didn't care. She refused to be formal and remote with him when he was to be her brother-in-law.

Clad once again in his coat and hat, Jeremiah left, followed soon after by Doc and his wife. Tom said he wanted to borrow some medical books and went with them.

Even as the front door closed, Grandpa covered a yawn. "If you don't mind, I think I'll leave you young folks to yourselves. A nap sounds mighty good to me right about now."

"Do you feel all right?" Concerned, Sarah placed a hand on his forearm.

"I'm fine, my girl. I've just got a full stomach, and a lie-down is what I need." He looked at Warren. "Glad you could join us after all, son. Not good when anger keeps a body away from church and from those who care about them."

Warren gave an abrupt nod.

Grandpa glanced at Sarah again. It seemed he wanted to say something more to her, but instead, he turned and went up the stairs to his room.

"What was that meeting about?" Warren asked as soon as they were alone. "Between your grandfather and Jeremiah."

"I assume it was because your brother's going to be the new deputy."

"What?"

Letting out a breath, she moved to the sofa and sat. "Jeremiah talked to Grandpa about it on Friday, and he was supposed to give his answer today."

"Why didn't you tell me?"

"Because it's sheriff's business." That was true enough. But not the whole truth. She hadn't wanted to tell Warren. *That* was the whole truth.

"I'm sorry we quarreled this morning," he said, his voice low and gruff. He sounded anything but sorry.

"I'm sorry too."

He drew a breath. "I'd better go."

Yes, she wished he would go. She walked to the entry. As she passed the round table, she grabbed his hat and turned to offer it to him.

She wasn't sure how it happened, but suddenly she was in his arms. He pulled her tight, crushing his hat between them. His mouth captured hers, hard and demanding. They'd kissed before over the months since their engagement, but nothing like this. In the past, Warren had lightly kissed her cheek or brushed his lips across hers, there and gone. This was different, and she struggled against him, pushing on his chest until he broke his hold.

She put a hand over her mouth as she took another step away from him. "What were you thinking?"

"I'm thinking that you're going to be my wife. I'm thinking that very soon you'll promise to love, honor, and obey me. I'm thinking you ought to obey me now, even before we marry."

She blinked, and only then did she realize there were tears in her eyes.

"I'll go." He grabbed his coat off the rack. "I'll see you for lunch on Tuesday." The words sounded part statement, part question.

She nodded, not sure what else to do.

He opened the door and looked back at her, his gaze challenging, then left.

She returned to the sofa in the parlor, trying to sort out her feelings. Feelings that had begun to frighten and confuse her.

EIGHT

Jeremiah was sworn in as the new deputy shortly before noon on Monday. After a few words of congratulations, the mayor and the sheriff left him alone in the office.

Deputy West. Now that was something. Last summer, when he'd stood on that battlefield and thought about returning to Boulder Creek, he'd never imagined this would be the result.

He turned to survey the room.

Off to his right was a scarred desk, its top littered with papers. In front of the desk sat two buckeye arm chairs with cane seats. Behind the desk was a large-armed chair with a high back and a swivel seat. A gun rack took up most of the corner behind and to the left of the desk. It held several Winchesters and two Colt rifles. A couple of oil paintings—one of bright sunflowers, the other of a family picnicking beside a stream—hung on the wall. Jeremiah wondered which female in the sheriff's life had chosen them. Probably his now-deceased wife since they looked as if they'd been on that wall for a couple of decades—and had rarely been dusted.

At the back of the room, near the door leading to the two jail cells, sat a Windsor wood stove, belching heat into the room. A blue-speckled coffee pot that had seen better days seemed to beckon to Jeremiah from atop the stove. He stepped to the sideboard and took one of the tin cups from a nook, then filled it with coffee. His first sip found the brew was dark and bitter. Frowning, he wondered when the pot had last been washed.

He returned to the desk and stacked the papers into a tidy pile, setting them on one corner. That looked better. He took another sip of the rapidly cooling coffee. *Ugh.* That wasn't better. It tasted as dreadful as before.

Putting the cup aside, he reached for the stack of papers. Wanted posters, for the most part. Slowly, he looked through them, noting the names, the crimes, the drawings.

"Hello, Jeremiah."

He looked up as Sarah entered the office. She wore a gray cloak with a fur-lined hood that draped gracefully over her hair. On one arm, she carried a wicker basket covered with a red-and-white-checked cloth.

She held the basket forward. "I've brought your lunch."

Jeremiah rose.

"Don't look so displeased, Deputy West. I haven't come to poison you."

"Sorry. I was surprised, that's all. Didn't expect food to be brought in."

"Like my grandmother before me, I always bring lunch to the sheriff or his deputy. And prisoners, too, when there are any."

"It's kind of you."

She pushed the hood from her head, then walked toward him, setting the basket on the desk. After spreading the checkered cloth over the papers, she set out a sandwich, a jar of applesauce, and another jar of milk.

"Looks good."

"Leftover beef from yesterday. But the bread was fresh-baked this morning." She took a step backward, as if to go.

He wished she wouldn't leave so soon and searched for something to say that might keep her here awhile longer.

"You can leave the basket and everything here. Grandpa will bring it home later. He always does a walk through town in the evening. Last thing he does is lock up the sheriff's office."

Jeremiah nodded.

She pulled up her hood, covering her hair once again. "Warren didn't even want the farm. Why is he so angry with you?"

His gut tightened. "I don't know. Wish I did. I don't know him. Not really. He was a little kid when I left Boulder Creek."

She looked away a second time. "And the two of you became very different men." She said the words softly, as if to herself rather than him.

"Yeah, I suppose we did."

Once again, she met his gaze. "I'll do whatever I can to help. I don't want the two of you to be estranged. It isn't how it should be between brothers."

"Warren's a lucky man. To have a woman who understands that."

Color rose in her cheeks. Ducking her head, she turned and left, cold air sweeping into the office before the door could close again.

"He's a very lucky man."

CONFUSION ROILED INSIDE SARAH AS SHE FOLLOWED THE BOARDWALK toward Warren's carpentry shop. When she left home, she hadn't intended to see him. But something about those few minutes in the sheriff's office made her want to mend things with her intended. He'd been angry yesterday, unreasonable. But he should know that Jeremiah wanted to heal whatever rift existed between them.

She frowned. Warren could be stubborn. Once he'd made up his mind, it was difficult for him to change it. And he was a creature of habit, so set in his ways. He ate his supper with the McNeals on Wednesdays and Saturdays and joined them for dinner on Sundays after church. On Tuesdays, he and Sarah ate lunch at the Randolph Hotel. Warren always ordered the fried chicken. Always. He worked in his carpentry shop from eight o'clock in the morning until six o'clock at night, six days a week. Except for Tuesdays, he allowed himself no more than thirty minutes for lunch. On Tuesdays, when they went to the hotel restaurant, he allowed a generous forty-five minutes.

She remembered his parting kiss the previous day. It had... It had frightened her in a way she didn't understand.

It didn't feel like love. It felt...wrong.

She stopped walking.

Warren had never said he loved her. Not in those precise words. But why else would he have waited so many years to marry her? Why else would he have pursued her? He must love her. No, he wasn't that mysterious count or duke of her girlhood dreams, but he was a good man. He would never defy convention as his brother had. He was an upstanding member of the community. He was fair and honest in his business dealings. He was industrious and would be a good provider for his wife and family.

A family. Children with Warren.

A shiver that had little to do with the cold ran up her spine.

She knew there was more than kissing needed for the begetting of children. But if she didn't want his kisses, however would she want more?

"Love grows the longer you're with a man," her grandmother had told her. "Your feelings for Warren will get stronger. You'll see."

But what if—

"Sarah?"

She blinked, the sound of Warren's voice drawing her from those troubled thoughts.

"What are you doing out here in the cold?"

"I...I came to see you." She'd been so lost in thought she hadn't realized she'd arrived at his shop.

"Come inside." Warren took hold of her elbow and drew her with him.

The shop smelled of fresh cut wood. Shavings littered the floor near the work bench.

"Whatever you wanted to talk about could have waited until tomorrow." He gave her a tolerant smile. "But if it's that important, we should sit down so you can tell me what's on your mind." He led the way to a pair of chairs.

She felt like a recalcitrant child, about to be reprimanded. Why was that?

Jeremiah doesn't make me feel like a child.

Warmth rose in her face, and she was thankful for the dim light.

"Now tell me what was so important it couldn't wait until tomorrow."

"I came about Jeremiah."

His mouth thinned. "Didn't we say enough about him yesterday?"

"He was sworn in as deputy this morning."

"So I understand."

"He wants the two of you to be on good terms."

"How do you know?"

"Because he told me. I promised to do what I could to mend the rift between you."

"When did he say that?"

"Just a short while ago."

"You were alone with him? Even after I told you to stay away from him."

She sat straighter, tilting her chin. "I always take lunch to the jail. Just like my grandmother before me."

"This is different."

She drew a long, slow breath and released it. "You're right. This is different. He's your brother." She rose from the chair. "And you should do whatever you can to make things right." She gave him a long look, then turned and left the shop.

CHAPTER
NINE

Jeremiah put the two empty jars into the basket and covered them with the checkered cloth. If he had his way, he would return the basket to the McNeal home himself, but he didn't have to think long on that thought to know why he shouldn't. He wanted to see Sarah again. He wanted to spend time with her. Being with her made him feel good. Made him feel...whole.

The door opened, and Jeremiah looked up from the basket to see Warren enter the office. His more pleasant thoughts skittered away.

"I understand Sarah came to see you." Warren stepped toward the desk.

"She brought the deputy lunch."

"It was more than that, and we both know it. It's important to her that we make peace with one another."

"Yes."

Warren glanced around the office. "I never pictured you as a deputy. Especially not in Boulder Creek."

"I never pictured it either."

"It wasn't fair, you know. Dad should've left the farm to me. I was the one who stayed. It should have been mine." His gaze returned to meet Jeremiah's. "I was the one who helped him till and plant and harvest all those years you were away."

"I know."

"I hated farming." Bitterness filled Warren's voice. "I always hated it, but I did it. But it didn't matter what I did for him. It was you he thought about. Even when we were little, it was always you. You were his favorite."

His favorite? Jeremiah almost laughed. He was the failure, not the favorite.

"He scrimped and saved because he wanted you to go to college, but there was never any money for me, for what I wanted to do." He leaned forward. "I was glad when you ran off. I thought maybe..." He let his words die away.

Strange, wasn't it, how two people remembered things? Jeremiah remembered a father who'd told him what a disappointment he was. He remembered the lectures, the whippings. His memories were of a man who never showed affection or approval. College money? If his dad put money away for that, he'd never said a word about it to Jeremiah.

Which one of the two sons recalled the real Ted West?

Warren had loved working with wood as a kid. He'd made the table that was still in the West house. He must have been about ten years old and already a craftsman. Jeremiah should have known his brother didn't want to be a farmer, that he'd rather be a carpenter.

Jeremiah, on the other hand, had always loved the land. Their dad had farmed out of necessity, as a way to feed his family, but Jeremiah had loved the look and the smell of the earth when it was freshly turned. He'd loved watching the green sprouts come up through the dark soil. He'd loved harvest time when a man could see what his hard labor and nature's blessings had wrought.

"Dad sent the money he saved to Marta's grandmother in Ohio, to help you two along. Wasn't much but it was all he had. He didn't keep one red cent of it for us. Not a penny."

Jeremiah's eyes widened.

Warren nodded. "It's true. As soon as he found out where the two of you went, he sent that money to help out."

"Grandma Ashmore gave me some money, but she didn't say where it came from. I thought it was hers." He drew a deep breath. "I'm sorry, Warren."

"You weren't supposed to know Dad sent it. He didn't want you to know." His brother rose and walked to the opposite end of the office, then back to the desk. "Sarah's going to be my wife. I've waited a long time for her. We don't always think alike, but I suppose she's right about you and me. Maybe we'll never be close, like Sarah and Tom are, but we should do our best to get along."

"I'd like that." Jeremiah rose, and they shook hands across the desk.

Warren didn't hold on long. He released Jeremiah's hand and took a step back. "I'd best go. I've got an order to fill by Friday." He paused, then added, "Sarah will expect you to join us for supper on Wednesday evenings."

"I don't want to intrude."

"You'd best plan on it."

After Warren left, Jeremiah sat once again and felt a small portion of the peace he'd sought fall into place. And he had Sarah McNeal to thank for it.

"CARE TO TELL ME WHAT'S TROUBLING YOU, PRINCESS?"

61

Sarah twisted on the window seat and met her grandfather's gaze as he entered through the open doorway of her bedroom. A heavy sigh escaped through parted lips. "I quarreled with Warren again."

Grandpa sat on a nearby chair. "Something serious?"

"About his brother."

His eyes narrowed. "It's more than that, I think."

She shook her head, but the denial was a lie. What worried her was the way she felt—or didn't feel—about Warren. Only how could she confess that to her grandfather when her wedding day was little more than two weeks away?

"Come downstairs and beat me at a game of checkers. Now that I've got a deputy again, I don't know what to do with myself. I'm as good as retired. Won't be long before I give up the badge altogether."

"Do you mind terribly?" She slipped off the window seat. "Retiring, I mean."

Grandpa stood and put an arm around her shoulders as she slid her own arm around his back. "No, I reckon I don't mind much. Just seems strange, is all."

"Maybe I should teach you how to cook."

He chuckled. "Not if you don't want the house burned down around your ears. Your grandma banished me from the kitchen when we were newlyweds. Said I could burn bread by just looking at it."

Sarah laughed. "Then no lessons. Grandma knew best."

She took her grandfather's hand, and the two of them went downstairs. Half an hour later, she was jumping a checker over one of his when she heard the front door open.

"It's me," her brother called from the entry. When he appeared at the parlor doorway, he added, "Look who I brought with me."

Jeremiah stepped to Tom's side, the wicker basket in one hand.

"I know you said to leave this at the jail, but I wanted to say thanks again."

She rose. "It was only a sandwich."

"Thanks for more than that."

Grandpa stood and greeted Jeremiah, then abruptly said, "Tom, there's something I need to show you in my study."

Tom glanced between Jeremiah and Sarah. "Sure thing." He followed their grandfather out of the parlor.

Strange, how the room seemed to narrow. She felt Jeremiah's presence like a physical touch. A feeling that made her want to draw closer to him. Instead, she moved away.

He took a step forward but stopped while there was still plenty of distance separating them. "I wanted to thank you for what you've done." A stray lock of his dark hair fell across his forehead, and he brushed at it with his fingertips.

She wished she could help him. She wanted to touch his face and brush his hair away. "What I've done?"

"Yes, for Warren and me. He came to see me this afternoon. I think things will be better between us in the future. Thanks to you."

She sank onto the sofa. "I'm glad I could help." She looked up, and her heart began to race.

"Warren told me he's waited a long time to marry you."

"He did?"

"Love's worth waiting for."

But does he love me? Will I love him? I don't think so. It feels wrong.

Jeremiah took a step backward, as if to leave.

"You loved your wife very much," she said softly.

It took several heartbeats before he answered. "Yes, I loved Marta."

"Two people loving each other. That's a wonderful thing."

Something flickered in his dark eyes. Something she wanted to understand but didn't.

After a lengthy silence, he said, "I need to get on my way."

"Yes. Of course." She stood. "Thanks for returning the basket. I...I'll see you tomorrow. Hot soup's on the menu."

He smiled. "I look forward to it."

CHAPTER

TEN

Two days later, Jeremiah stood in the doorway of the farmhouse. A sharp wind whistled beneath the eaves while dark clouds roiled and churned across the heavens, bringing with them the promise of more snow.

The long ride to and from town, morning and night, was unpleasant enough in the cold. It was worse when there was snow on the ground, and it looked to him as if there would be plenty of that this week. Maybe plenty of it for the next few months if it stayed this cold.

Yesterday the sheriff had suggested Jeremiah turn the storeroom above the jail into a place to stay when the weather didn't cooperate. Looked to him like the older man was right. Jeremiah didn't want to get stuck out here on the farm when he'd been hired to do a job in town. And since he didn't have any other livestock that needed tending, staying in Boulder Creek during the winter made good sense.

He closed the door and went to the stove where he stoked the fire. As soon as the chill was gone from the air and the water in the kettle was warm, he washed and shaved. A short while later, dressed for the day, he prepared breakfast, his thoughts returning to that empty storeroom.

He would need a bed, a small table, and one chair. Maybe Warren would help him with those. He could buy other necessities—like a couple of blankets and a pillow—at the mercantile. He could eat at one of the town's two restaurants, except for supper on Wednesdays and Saturdays. He was expected at the McNeal house on those nights, as well as Sunday after church.

Remembering that brought Sarah to mind. He pictured her as he'd last seen her. Hair swept up from her slender neck, loose tendrils coiling at the nape. Blue eyes fringed by thick lashes. A smile bowing her lips.

She'd been kind and welcoming to him from the day they met. She'd said she remembered both him and Marta, but he couldn't say the same. Why would he remember her? She would have been only about seven or eight when he left Boulder Creek. Just another little girl on the playground of the schoolyard.

She wasn't a little girl any longer. She was a woman. A beautiful, refined woman.

He frowned as he sat at the table with his breakfast.

She's your brother's bride-to-be.

He felt the words like a rock in his gut. He tried to tell himself it was because he needed to think of Sarah like a sister. But he wasn't much good at lying, not even to himself. His thoughts were anything but brotherly.

He pushed the plate of fried eggs away, his appetite gone.

Even if Sarah hadn't been engaged to his brother, he wouldn't welcome this pull of attraction toward her. He'd been married. He'd loved and lost. He'd watched his wife and child die. He wouldn't risk having that happen again. He was single and meant to stay single.

He slid the chair back from the table. He'd better get a move on if he wanted to get to town before snow started to fall.

MID-MORNING, SARAH ENTERED THE DRESS SHOP, PUSHED FROM behind by a blast of frigid air.

"Good gracious!" Madeline Gaunt waved her hands. "Hurry and close the door, my dear, before we both catch our deaths." The petite, bird-like woman bustled forward, put her arm around Sarah, and ushered her toward the back of the shop where a stove belched heat into the rest of the room.

"You take off your coat while I get some tea to warm you."

"I'm all right, Mrs. Gaunt. Really. The walk from home isn't that far."

"If I'd known it'd be this cold, I'd have settled in Texas," the woman muttered as she filled a cup from the tea kettle. "An old woman like me belongs in milder climates."

"You're not old."

"I am, and don't you deny me the right to say so, young lady. I worked hard to get to this age." Madeline folded her hands over her stomach. "Now, you sit while the tea steeps."

Sarah obeyed.

"You won't believe how much I've accomplished these past two weeks, my dear. This is going to be my most beautiful creation ever." As she spoke, the seamstress entered the back room. When she came out, she carried Sarah's bridal gown across her arm. "Thank heaven you decided on a long engagement. Sewing on these iridescent beads has been the most difficult task of all." Madeline motioned for Sarah to join her. "Forget the tea. Your wedding day is nearly upon us. You don't have time to lounge about."

Laughter burbled up in Sarah's throat, but seeing the

woman's serious expression made her swallow it back as she stood.

A short while later, she stared at her reflection in the looking glass. The *princesse* style gown was made of the finest satin. The bodice had a high neck, and a lacy fichu was caught at the waist with a silver pin. The three-quarter sleeves had enormous puffs that seemed to broaden her shoulders and narrow her waist.

"Oh, my!" Madeline pressed her palms together in front of her mouth. "I had no idea. You were so right to choose this pattern. It's breathtaking, even if I do say so myself. What a beautiful bride you shall be."

Sarah almost burst into tears. She'd never worn anything this lovely in her life—and she'd never felt this miserable either.

Madeline reached for her pins. "Let me make a few adjustments. A tuck here and there is all it needs. Now don't move. I don't want to poke you."

A FEW HOURS LATER, AS SARAH STOOD IN HER OWN KITCHEN preparing supper, she couldn't hold back the tears. They ran down her cheeks, blinding her to the knife in one hand and the partially chopped onion on the counter.

"Hey, what's wrong?" Tom asked from the doorway.

For a moment, she didn't know what to say. She couldn't tell him how much she dreaded her wedding day, that she was more and more unhappy at the thought of it.

"Sis?" He took a step closer.

Blinking, she held up the knife. "Onions. They make my eyes water." She sniffed. "Here. You chop them." She put the knife down and turned her back to him. As she moved toward the stove, she wiped her eyes with the hem of her apron.

"You can tell me anything, you know." Tom's voice was low and gentle.

"There's nothing to tell."

"I'm smarter than I look, Sarah."

She smiled, despite her tears, and faced him again. "You look smart, too."

"Do I?" He gave her a cheeky grin.

"Yes."

He sobered. "If you won't tell me what's troubling you, tell someone else. Grandpa or one of the ladies at church. How about Skylark James? Or Rosalie Randolph? They'd be glad to listen and help if they could."

"There's nothing to tell," she repeated.

She was a poor liar. She could see that in his sympathetic eyes.

"What've you got on the stove?"

"Stew."

"And in the oven?"

"Bread."

"I'll add the onions to the stew and keep an eye on the bread. You run upstairs, wash your face, and put on your favorite dress. We'll make a party out of tonight. No more sad thoughts for the rest of the night. Sound good?"

She nodded, her throat tight. Then she hurried out of the kitchen to do as he'd suggested.

CHAPTER
ELEVEN

Tom did manage to turn the evening into a party. He regaled his family and the friends around the supper table with a recitation of his escapades at boarding school. Time and again, the dining room rang with laughter, and by the time Sarah served dessert, her mood had brightened. She was blessed, and she knew it. She had no reason to be sad.

I mustn't want what God doesn't want for me.

Her gaze fell upon Warren. He was an upstanding member of the community. He wouldn't spoil her the way her grandfather had, but he would be good to her. Perhaps he didn't love her the way the hero of her daydreams would have, but love like that—butterflies and breathlessness and swooning—wasn't real. That was a romanticized love taken from novels. She was about to turn twenty-two. Time to put away childish things, as the Good Book said.

"Tell me, Jeremiah." Grandpa's deep voice intruded on her thoughts. "Did you get settled in today?"

"Yes, sir."

"Settled in?" Warren asked, looking at his brother.

"Until the weather changes, I'll be staying in town."

Warren's brows drew together in a frown. "Where?"

"In the storage room over the jail."

Grandpa nodded. "I'm thankful he'll be close at hand, in case he's needed."

"The old storeroom," Tom said with a shake of his head. "Behind the false front. I forgot it was there." He glanced at Sarah. "Remember when we hid up there because we'd eaten most of that cake Grandma'd baked for the church supper. We knew we were going to be in a world of trouble."

Sarah laughed softly. "The whole town was out looking for us for hours. I thought Grandma would skin us alive when we finally came out of hiding. She made Grandpa put a lock on that door after that." She moved her gaze to Jeremiah. "I can't imagine living there in the winter. Won't you be cold? And there's only that slit of a window."

"I don't need much. Just a place to sleep."

There was something in the dark depths of his eyes that told her he'd slept in worse places. Places she wouldn't be able to imagine. For a moment, she saw beyond his eyes and into his heart. She recognized pain and loneliness, and she felt it as if it were her own. She lowered her gaze to her plate, an odd ache in her chest stealing her breath.

Chair legs scraped the floor, and Jeremiah said, "I'd better see to my rounds." He stood.

Grandpa chuckled. "There's another reason I'm glad you're staying in town. I don't have to do evening rounds."

After a nod to her grandfather, Jeremiah looked at Sarah. "Supper was delicious."

"You're always welcome."

Something flickered in his eyes. A response that was there and gone.

Warren pushed back his chair and rose. "It's time I was going, as well. Mind if I walk with you, Jeremiah?"

"If you want."

Warren moved to Sarah's place at the table and took hold of her hand. He squeezed her fingers. "Good night, Sarah."

He didn't bend to kiss her cheek as some men were wont to do. Warren thought public displays of affection unacceptable. He'd told her so more than once. But then she recalled the forceful way he'd kissed her a few days earlier, a kiss that had frightened her and...repelled her.

Repelled?

A chill passed along her spine.

Warren bid goodnight to Tom and Grandpa, then followed Jeremiah out of the dining room. Moments later, the front door opened, then closed as the brothers left the house.

I don't love him. I don't want to marry him.

It didn't matter to her that Warren had many good qualities. It didn't matter that other young women in Boulder Creek thought she was lucky that he'd waited for her to accept his proposal. His *multiple* proposals.

I don't want to be his wife.

The wedding was barely two weeks away. Whatever was she to do?

JEREMIAH AND WARREN WALKED IN SILENCE UNTIL THEY REACHED THE corner of Main and North. Once there, Warren stopped, forcing Jeremiah to do the same.

After clearing his throat, Warren said, "I've waited a long time to make Sarah my wife."

"You're a lucky man."

"I was about eighteen when she caught my eye, and I knew

one day I would make her mine. She is beautiful, of course, but she also comes from a fine family. A businessman must have the right kind of wife to succeed."

Darkness blanketed the town, and the moonless evening hid Warren's features from Jeremiah. But something in his brother's words didn't sit right with him. There was no note of affection in what he'd said about Sarah.

What about love? He swallowed the question, knowing he didn't have a right to ask it.

Warren began walking again, and Jeremiah fell in beside him.

"I suppose you know we plan to live in the McNeal house after we're married."

"No. I don't think I'd heard it."

"Hank McNeal's getting up there in years, and Tom will be off to school, so it just makes sense. And there are plenty of bedrooms, so there'll be room for children when they come along." There was a pause, then, "Do you plan to make any changes to the house out at the farm?"

"Hadn't thought about it." Lamplight spilled out through the windows of the Pony Saloon. Men played cards at one table. More stood at the bar, nursing drinks. A couple of fancy women mingled with the male patrons. Tinny music from the piano slipped past the closed doors.

"You ought to make improvements. The place'd be worth more with a bigger house on it."

"I'm not planning to sell so it doesn't much matter what it's worth."

"Won't you marry again? It's not big enough for a wife and family. At least that's what it felt like to me when we were growing up."

"I don't plan on marrying again." His reply was sharp, and

he hoped his brother would take the hint. This was not a topic he wanted to discuss.

It worked. They completed the walk to the carpentry shop in silence. Warren opened the door and went inside with a quick, "Good night."

Jeremiah turned. Across the street, the Randolph Hotel looked festive with lights shining through many windows. In the nearby boarding house, only the parlor was aglow, and Carson's Barber Shop and Bath House was darkened for the night.

A quiet night in Boulder Creek.

He made his way back along Main Street until he reached the sheriff's office. Inside, he stoked the stove, then climbed the stairs to the storage room. A bedroll awaited him on the floor, but it wouldn't be the first time he'd slept in a cold room without a bed. He stripped down to his long underwear and got beneath the top two blankets.

The wind had risen again, and it sang a mournful tune on its way through town. Jeremiah rolled onto his left side and draped an arm over his right ear, trying to block the sound.

"Won't you marry again?"

Warren's question repeating in his mind was worse than the wind. Jeremiah couldn't expect his brother to understand. Warren had never failed to protect the woman he loved, the woman he'd vowed to provide for. But Jeremiah knew that loss all too well. He'd tried to be a good husband, but in the end he'd failed Marta. His poor decisions had cost his wife her life, along with that of their child.

He rolled onto his other side and pulled the blankets up over his head. Then, unbidden and unwanted, the image of Sarah came into his mind. Sarah with hair that seemed to invite a man's fingers to caress it. Sarah with eyes like pieces of sky. Sarah with an innocence that was at once frightening and provocative. Sarah...who belonged to Warren.

He squeezed his eyes more tightly closed. If he'd wanted proof that the better part of him had died with Marta, this was it. A better man wouldn't think this way about his own brother's bride-to-be.

"What am I doing here?" he whispered into the darkness. "Maybe I shouldn't have come back."

CHAPTER
TWELVE

J eremiah tromped through the fresh layer of snow on his way back to the jail from the telegraph office. In his first week as a sheriff's deputy, he'd found there was paperwork even when there was no trouble. It had come as a surprise that he found much of it interesting. Certainly more than assembling motors in a factory or laying railroad tracks. And while he didn't much care for the cold, it still beat living in an army tent in the tropics, being eaten alive by mosquitos.

He opened the door to the sheriff's office, then stamped his feet a time or two to shake loose the snow before stepping inside. When he looked up, he found Sarah in a chair near the desk, the familiar picnic basket with its red-and-white-checked cloth on the floor beside her.

She smiled. "I wondered where you'd gone."

Sarah had brought him lunch every day this week, and yet it still surprised him, seeing her sitting there. Heaven help him.

"I brought your lunch," she added softly—as if he wouldn't know why she was there.

He shrugged out of his coat and hung it on a hook near the

door. "So I see."

"My grandfather sent a message."

Jeremiah walked around to the other side of the desk. "And what's that?"

"He noticed you still don't have much upstairs. He wants you to have a mattress we've got in the attic. And we have a couple of spare lamps, too."

"That's kind of him." He sat.

Sarah lifted the basket from the floor and set it on the desk. "It's cold sandwiches again and a jar of peaches. There are a few cookies as well. I'm trying a new recipe for the Christmas social on Saturday. I hope you like them."

"I like everything you make."

Her cheeks colored as she lowered her gaze.

"This is real kind for you to do every day. But you know I could eat lunch at the hotel restaurant or at Zoe's."

"Don't be silly. This is what the McNeal women do." She glanced toward the window and back again. "Besides, I know you took this job so you could pay Warren for the farm. You didn't have to do that. You don't owe him. Your father left the farm to you. It's yours."

"Maybe I owe him. Maybe I don't." He frowned. "Paying him a share will help the two of you get started after the wedding." The words left a bad taste in his mouth.

Something flickered across Sarah's face. An expression that Jeremiah couldn't discern. Unhappiness? Seemed unlikely.

"Besides, there's nothing much I can do out at the farm until the spring thaw. You won't see me in town often after that."

"I hope you'll still come for supper sometimes."

He gave her a fleeting smile. "You won't want me under foot."

"You're wrong. You'll always be welcome."

He knew better. Warren wouldn't want him coming for suppers on a regular basis. Even if he and his brother were able to become friends after all these years, a man would rather spend time alone with his wife. Jeremiah wouldn't be welcome.

Hoping to change the subject, he asked, "Are you and Warren taking a wedding trip? I haven't heard any mention of it."

"We thought we would go back east. To Philadelphia and New York. But I don't think we will."

"You must be disappointed. Why the change?"

She shrugged. "The time wasn't right."

He wished he could drive out her disappointment. He wished he could give her what would make her happy.

Disquieted by the thoughts, he lifted the sandwich from the basket. "I never found much to my liking in the East." He took a bite of the bread, ham, and cheese.

"Really? The *Ladies' Home Journal* has had many stories about Philadelphia and New York. It all seems so...so exciting and wonderful."

He set down the sandwich. "Maybe it is wonderful for the rich of society. But most people in those big cities live in rat-infested tenements. They work in factories where they roast in the summer and freeze in the winter, and they die without most anybody knowing or caring. Nobody writes about that in the *Ladies' Home Journal*."

Her beautiful eyes widened.

He shouldn't have said anything. He should have let her keep her fantasies. "Sorry."

"Jeremiah, don't you have any good memories about the years you were away?"

"Yes. A few."

Her expression softened. "Tell me about her. Tell me about

79

Marta."

A part of him wanted to do as she asked. A part of him wanted to tell her all the joys and sorrows he'd shared with Marta. Marta hadn't been physically beautiful like Sarah, but her heart had been big enough to take in the whole world. She had loved Jeremiah and had made him a better man because of it. But there was another part of him that refused to talk about her with Sarah. He didn't know why. He just couldn't do it. Maybe with someone else. Not with Sarah McNeal.

His appetite gone, he stood. "I've got things to see to." His words sounded abrupt in his own ears.

She blinked, almost as if to hold back tears. Then she rose, too. "I'm sorry for prying. I didn't mean to."

"It's not that. I have business to take care of." Like a coward, he remained behind his desk as she left the office.

As the door closed, he realized why he didn't want to talk about Marta with her. It was because Sarah had opened a door in his heart—only a crack, but an opening nonetheless—and he feared what that might mean for the future.

SARAH PULLED THE CLOAK TIGHT ABOUT HER AS SHE HURRIED TOWARD home. She kept her gaze fastened on the snowy path beneath her feet. Partly to be careful not to slip and fall. But mostly because she didn't want to see anyone else, didn't want to chance another conversation.

She'd wanted to stay in that office with Jeremiah. She'd wanted him to tell her about the life he'd had with Marta. She'd wanted to understand the love they'd shared.

Perhaps her expectations had been influenced by romantic novels and girlish daydreams, but her heart told her that she wasn't wrong to want more than what she felt for Warren. No matter what her grandmother had said, she wanted to begin marriage already in love with her husband. She wanted to eagerly await his kisses, not dread them.

What would it be like to kiss Jeremiah?

Her heart fluttered at the silent question.

I must tell Warren I can't marry him.

She stopped walking.

I must tell him soon.

She'd let it go on far too long. Grandpa had asked her what was wrong. Tom had asked her what was wrong. She'd lied to them both. She'd pretended all was well. But it was anything but well. It was a disaster. Warren had to be told. She couldn't avoid hurting him.

But would he even be hurt?

She looked down Main Street. She couldn't see all the way to the carpentry shop. Other buildings blocked her view. But she knew where it was. She knew Warren would be inside the shop, cutting or sanding or varnishing a chair or a bed or a table. But would he be thinking about her? Something inside told her it was unlikely. Warren was a singularly focused man.

No, he wouldn't be hurt when she broke the engagement because his heart had never been invested in the union. His pride might be wounded. He might resent her for altering his plans. But he wouldn't be heartbroken. He wouldn't suffer in that way.

Her gaze shifted toward the sheriff's office, and in her mind she saw Jeremiah as he'd been minutes ago. He had loved Marta enough to defy his father. He'd married Marta. He'd built a life with her. And losing his wife had cost him more than Sarah was able to comprehend.

I want to be loved like that.

She turned toward home again. "I don't want to give up on that dream," she whispered. "Not ever."

THIRTEEN

For the first time in over two weeks, Friday dawned with a light cloud cover and the temperature above freezing. It was a good day for a trek to find the perfect Christmas tree.

Bundled in her warmest, fur-lined cloak, a hood covering her head and her hands tucked into a fur muff, Sarah left the mercantile and hurried along the boardwalk toward the hotel. She'd reached the livery stable when the oversized door opened, and Jeremiah rode out astride a large buckskin. He reined in when he saw her. The gelding snorted and bobbed his head impatiently, breath making tiny clouds beneath his nostrils.

Sarah's heart did a tiny skip at the sight of man and horse. They seemed a well-suited pair, both of them powerful and restive. She hadn't realized it until now, but she'd hoped to see him this morning and had watched for him as she'd walked through town.

"Morning, Sarah." He touched the brim of his hat.

She offered a tiny smile. "Good morning, Jeremiah. Are you

on your way out of town?" It was a silly question. Why else would he be on horseback?

"Out to the farm. I need to bring back a few more things."

"I'm going with the Randolphs for Christmas trees. We'll go by your farm on our way to the mountains. You're welcome to ride with us if you'd like."

Something flickered in his eyes. The wish to accept her invitation?

Emboldened, she added, "We'll decorate the tree for the Christmas social as soon as we get back. You'll be there, won't you? At the social tomorrow."

"Hadn't thought about it."

"You would be missed."

The hint of a smile tipped the corners of his mouth. "I'll be there."

Perhaps he would ask her to dance. Perhaps he would take her in his arms for a waltz while an orchestra played Tchaikovsky or Strauss. She could almost see a glorious chandelier overhead, ablaze with light. She could imagine Jeremiah wearing a fine suit and gloves. She could see herself in a satin gown with a long train and—

"Sarah."

She heard Warren's voice but was reluctant to turn away from Jeremiah, reluctant to let the daydream fade away. She wanted to savor these strange, unfamiliar feelings that coursed through her whenever she was with him.

"Sarah!"

Frustrated, she turned.

"Couldn't you hear me calling you?" Warren strode toward her.

"I'm sorry."

He gave Jeremiah a nod of acknowledgement, then

returned his gaze to her. "You'd better come along. The Randolphs are ready to leave. They're waiting for you."

Jeremiah said, "I'd best be on my way."

Wanting to object, Sarah looked at the man on horseback again.

"Hope you find the perfect trees." Jeremiah bent the brim of his hat, then rode away from the couple.

"If you don't get going," Warren said, "you won't have time to get the trees you want, perfect or not."

"You're not coming?" She looked at him, relief washing over her. She'd dreaded spending the day with him. She needed to tell him that she couldn't marry him, but it needed to be at the right time and in the right way. This wasn't it.

He shook his head. "I'm taking the train down to Boise. I've got business there." He took hold of her arm and propelled her along the boardwalk. "You'd best hurry. The Randolph children are impatient."

She longed to plant her feet and refuse to go another step. She was tired of him giving her orders.

"You didn't ask why I'm going to Boise," he continued, failing to read her mood. "I've received a telegram from Mr. Kubicki. He wants to form a partnership. We're going to discuss the terms."

"What sort of partnership?"

"The merging of our businesses. You and I would need to live in the capital city, but it would be worth it. My business would double, even triple. It's an opportunity of a lifetime."

Now she planted her feet. "Leave Boulder Creek?"

"What's to keep us here? It's an opportunity too good to pass up."

"What's to keep us here?" she echoed softly. "Warren, this is our home. Grandpa is here. What about all your plans to fix up his house? I thought you wanted to live there and turn it into a showplace for your woodwork." She shook her head. "Isn't this something we should decide together? We need to talk about it."

"Don't worry. When I get back, you'll see this is what's best for us. And you'll have plenty of time to pack for a move to Boise. I doubt it will happen for a month or two. And since we postponed a wedding trip, this will be the perfect time to get ready for a move." He pulled her forward once again.

He hadn't heard her question about deciding about a move together. Either that or he didn't care what she thought. He believed he was right and that she would come around to his way of thinking in time.

Her grandmother had said a wife's place was at her husband's side, no matter what.

But I'm not his wife. I don't intend to be his wife.

Perhaps she would have changed her mind about when to break their engagement. Perhaps she would have told him, right then and there, that the wedding was off. But before she could open her mouth, she saw Michael Randolph. He stood beside the wagon, runners replacing wheels, his children and wife already seated in it.

"There you are." Michael waved. "Have you decided to join us, Warren?"

"Afraid not. Too much work to do. But I've brought Sarah along. Heaven knows when she would have arrived if I hadn't gone after her."

It's over, Warren. No matter what you say later, it is over now.

Jeremiah built a fire in the stove and stood near it, waiting for the room to warm, his thoughts on the young woman in a silver-gray cloak, white fur framing her face. He saw Sarah's sweet smile and heard her lovely voice. How he'd wanted to accept her invitation to ride with her and the Randolphs on their way out of town. He would have loved the company instead of the quiet, solitary ride. If Warren hadn't come along when he had, maybe—

She's Warren's girl.

But if so, what was this strange connection he felt with her? Was it merely because she'd been kind to him from the start? Or was it something more?

He rubbed a hand over his face and looked around the log house.

"Was I wrong to come back?" he asked the silence.

It wasn't the first time he'd wondered about his decision to return, but this time, something in his gut answered. He hadn't been wrong. This was where he was supposed to be. He didn't know how he knew. He just knew.

He glanced toward a small table near a second chair. His mother's Bible lay on it, closed, a layer of dust on its leather cover. He didn't remember much about his mother, but one image lingered in his mind. Of her sitting near the fireplace in their old home—the one where the West family lived before his mother died and his dad moved them to Boulder Creek— the Bible open on her lap, her lips sometimes moving in prayer.

Marta had been like that, too. She would sit with the Bible and read, squinting when the light was dim. Other times she would hold the book close to her chest, as if trying to take it in through her heart.

"I don't have the kind of faith they had."

He crossed to the table and took up the Bible. As in his memory of Marta, he pressed it to his chest.

"I could use that kind of faith. I'm tired of being without it."

He went to the chair near the stove and sat.

In a louder voice this time, he said, "I reckon we haven't talked much lately, Lord. Maybe it's time we did so."

And talk, he did.

As if God Almighty didn't already know the roads he'd traveled, Jeremiah told Him of the years after leaving Boulder Creek, of his love for his wife, of their excitement over the child she carried. He shared with God about the heartbreak when he'd lost Marta and their newborn son to the sickness that had swept through that small town in Ohio. He told of the years that followed, of his anger, his bitterness, the wish that he too could die and have the pain be over. He talked about the voice in his heart on San Juan Hill that had told him to come home. He told the Lord about Warren's anger, and finally, he confessed his attraction to Sarah McNeal. Not that he would act on feelings with her or any other woman, but the attraction was there all the same. He saw that clearly now and there was a measure of relief in admitting it.

Finally, when the words ran out, he fell asleep in the chair, the warmth from the fire wrapping him in a blanket of comfort.

When he awakened, the fire had burned down and the room lay in darkness. He rose, working a kink out of his neck with one hand, then walked to the window. Snow was falling again, and if he was any judge of the clouds, he would be better off spending tonight at the farm. Tomorrow was his day off, and there was no point pushing his horse through a storm when it wasn't necessary. Thankfully there was enough food here to see him through, even if the storm lingered a few days.

He slipped on his coat and headed to the barn. He'd left his mount saddled, never intending to stay more than thirty minutes or an hour. As he unsaddled the gelding, he wondered how long he'd been asleep. Minutes? Hours? He didn't know and the storm made it hard to tell time.

After putting hay into the feed bin, he patted the horse's neck. "I'll get you some water, fella."

At the barn door, he looked up through the curtain of falling snow and wondered if the Randolph party had returned to Boulder Creek with their Christmas trees. Must have. Michael wouldn't have been asleep like Jeremiah. He would have seen the storm rolling in and headed back to town, with or without the trees. They were most likely in Boulder Creek even now, seated beside a nice, warm fire. He intended to do the same.

FEAR SKITTERED IN SARAH'S HEART.

The snowstorm had begun—little more than a white lacy curtain—while she and the Randolph children were on the bobsled, sailing down a hillside.

"Let's do it again!" six-year-old Sophia had exclaimed the moment they'd reached the bottom.

Before Sarah answered, she'd looked upward and been surprised by the darkened sky. Something had told her the snowfall wouldn't remain lacy for long.

Perhaps thinking the same thing, Michael had called, "Let's go. Leave the sled. I'll come back for it another day."

How much time passed between the moment Sarah and the children had clambered into the bed of the wagon and now, she couldn't tell. The world had gone white. Sky and earth looked exactly the same. When she looked toward the wagon seat, she could barely make out Michael and Rosalie. How could Michael know if he drove the team in the right direction?

A strong gust of wind hit the wagon. A wailing sound, like the banshee of Irish legends, sent another wave of fear icing through her. She hugged the children to her sides, more for her own comfort than for theirs. The blinding snow stung her face, and she closed her eyes, dipped her head forward, and prayed they would be all right.

A moment later, the sleigh came to a halt.

"I'm getting down to lead the horses," Michael shouted. "Everybody stay put."

"I'm scared!" Sophia cried.

"Don't be," Sarah answered. "Your dad knows what he's doing."

The words were no more out of her mouth than the wagon bed tilted and slid sideways. Benjamin grunted as Sarah's and Sophia's weight knocked into him.

"Are you okay?" Sarah asked.

"Yeah." He didn't sound all right. He sounded frightened.

She pushed herself away from the wagon seat that had been at her back, letting Sophia slide into the empty spot. The wagon shifted again, and Sarah's heart rose in her throat.

"Rosalie," Michael shouted, "get down. Now!"

A horse's shrill whinny cut the air.

"Sarah, get the children over the side. Hurry."

The wagon tilted a little more.

Sarah fought against gravity. Instinct told her that if they went over the side that seemed closest to the ground, they might fall down a mountainside. Or worse, the wagon might topple over on top of them.

Again there came a piercing cry from one of the horses.

Somehow, she half led and half dragged the two children to the back of the wagon.

"I'm here," Rosalie called above the wail of the wind.

Sarah found her friend's hand on the rear of the wagon. She shoved Sophia toward her mother. "Here she is. Here's Sophia."

"I've got her."

Hands free again, Sarah pulled Benjamin into position so she could repeat the action with him. Rosalie returned, shouting to let Sarah know she was there. Sarah pushed Benjamin in the direction of his mother's voice. The wagon shuddered violently, and the boy slipped from her grasp.

"Rosalie?" she screamed above the wind.

Did Rosalie have him? *Please, God!*

The wagon gave a violent jerk. Sarah tried to catch herself, but her hand found nothing but air.

Another scream. Was it the horse again or was it Sarah herself? She couldn't be sure, for in the next instant she sailed free of the wagon. She flailed her arms, seeking purchase, but there was nothing solid to be found.

What seemed an eternity later, her flight was stopped. The breath whooshed from her lungs as she hit something hard and ungiving. But her relief was short lived as she began to tumble and roll. Down and down and down until blackness overtook her.

CHAPTER
FOURTEEN

When Sarah returned to her senses, she saw nothing but a curtain of white. Cold seeped through her cloak. Groaning, she struggled to a sitting position. Her muscles ached, but a quick examination told her nothing had been broken in her fall down the mountainside.

She cupped her hands around her mouth. "Michael! Rosalie!" Only the wind answered her. She turned her head one way, then the other, but she couldn't see more than a few feet away, if that.

Had Benjamin made it into his mother's arms? Had the wagon followed her down the mountain? Were the Randolphs on foot? Were they looking for her or seeking shelter from the blizzard?

God, please let Benjamin be all right. He was so frightened. Keep him safe. Keep them all safe.

She shivered and pulled her cloak more tightly about her, thankful that it hadn't been torn away during her fall. A miracle, she supposed. She struggled to her feet, testing her limbs once again. Bruised, perhaps, but no sprains. She could walk.

There were no cabins in this area that she knew of. She would have to get down to the valley in order to find one of the scattered farms and ranches. But that, too, would take a miracle.

"Michael! Rosalie!" She looked upward, listening, hoping. Still nothing but the wind for a reply.

Michael couldn't have remained where the wagon had begun its slide.

Unless Benjamin fell down the mountain, too.

Her heart raced as she turned in a slow circle, trying to decide what to do. She didn't know which way was up or down, backward or forward. She couldn't look for the little boy if she didn't know where to start.

"Michael! Rosalie! Benjamin!"

The wind whistled around her.

Be calm, Sarah. Think. Think!

Michael would have taken his family to safety. That would have been his first priority. He couldn't risk them while trying to find her. But others would come for her when they could. In the meantime, she must keep moving. She must try to find shelter. Any kind of shelter.

One arm outstretched, she took a step and then another, feeling her way, testing the ground, praying that it would remain solid beneath her, frightened every time it felt as if the earth went up instead of down.

Tears welled in her eyes. They were warm. How could her tears be warm when everything else about her was bitterly cold?

God, be with the Randolph family, and help me find my way.

HOLDING ONTO THE ROPE HE'D TIED BETWEEN THE HOUSE AND BARN, Jeremiah leaned into the wind as he went to check on his horse.

It had been years since he'd experienced a blizzard like this one. Heavy snows, yes. He'd seen plenty of those. But this world of white, sky and earth melding together? He'd only been in one storm like it. When he was in Montana working on a cattle ranch. And he would have been happy never to see the like again.

Once inside the barn, he removed his calvary hat and shook off the snow. "Hey, fella." Setting the hat on his head again, he crossed the hard-packed floor to the stall.

The gelding thrust his head over the top rail and snorted.

"Yeah, you don't like this weather either. But we'll be okay. Enough feed for both of us, even if the storm lasts." After a pat on the horse's neck, he went to the barrel holding oats and scooped some into a bucket.

His thoughts returned, as they often had throughout the afternoon, to Sarah and the Randolph family. "Hope they're as safe as we are."

The gelding buried his muzzle in the bucket and chomped, his hunger overcoming any unease caused by the storm. The barn wasn't what Jeremiah would call warm, but no ice had formed in the water bucket in the last few hours. Meaning the temperature was above freezing. More animals would have warmed the space even more. Come spring, he hoped there would be another horse or two along with a couple of cows. And at least one dog. Maybe even some cats to keep down the mice population.

A picture of his mom flashed in his head, one of her seated on the porch, a gray tabby cat curled in her lap. Was it an actual memory or only his imagination? He couldn't be sure.

He'd been a youngster when she passed, and his memories of her were few.

His dad hadn't believed in pets. Animals on a farm were meant to work or provide food or income. That meant dogs and cats too. But Jeremiah liked the idea of his mom holding a cat, petting it, listening to it purr. It brought a smile to his lips.

Yes, next summer, he would definitely get a cat or two to inhabit the barn.

Still smiling, he turned up the collar of his coat, pulled his hat low on his forehead, and ventured into the storm.

EXHAUSTION AND COLD PULLED AT SARAH AS SHE STUMBLED BLINDLY forward. It felt as if she'd walked for days. She'd tripped and fallen many times, and many times she'd had to force herself to rise again. It would have been so much easier to curl up on the ground and let the snow cover her like a blanket. Even a few moments of sleep would have been a relief. Somehow, every time she fell, she'd risen and kept going.

She was fairly certain the ground had leveled, that she had reached the valley floor. Only once had she found herself climbing again and had to correct her direction. She thought she'd walked in a straight line. But how could she know? She hadn't come upon Pony Creek as yet. Had she passed any farms or ranches without seeing the buildings? All she could see was white. Just white. So much white it hurt to keep her eyes open.

But even a heavy snowfall didn't remain a blinding white once the sun set, and when the blackness fell, terror made Sarah feel even colder than before.

Will I die this night?

Had the Randolphs made it back to town? Whether or not they had, Grandpa and Tom would be worried about her.

Would they be foolish enough to venture out in this storm in search of her?

Please, God, keep them safe. No matter what happens to me, don't let them come to harm.

She might have cried if the tears didn't feel frozen inside of her. She stumbled again and pitched forward. Her forehead hit something, and pain shot from her head and down her neck into her back. She cried out as she descended deeper into a drift. Seconds or minutes passed, and at last she sought something to hold onto to help her stand. That was when she understood what she'd fallen against.

Wood. A house? A barn? A shed?

She struggled to her feet and felt her way along the wall until she found a door. After lifting the latch, she gave it a push. It didn't budge. She tried again, this time pulling. The door tried to follow her, but only an inch or two. The snow. Of course. She needed to clear away the snow.

First, she leaned near the crack in the door and called, "Is anyone in there?" She could barely hear herself above the wind. No answer came. Something told her she wasn't breaking into a house, but an outbuilding. From the distance she'd followed before reaching a door, it must be a barn. This had to be a side door, for it was no bigger than the front door of the McNeal home. It wasn't big enough for a team of horses or a plow or wagon to pass through.

Dizziness swept over her as she bent to shovel snow with scooped hands. It was tempting to simply drop and rest. Could a few minutes matter?

Yes. Yes, even a few minutes was too much. She needed to get out of the storm.

One more time. Just sweep away a little more. Only a little more.

She tried the door again, and it opened a few more inches.

The success gave her a boost of energy. Her aching arms and hands moved a little faster, scooping and tossing and sweeping snow away, even as it continued to fall.

The next time she tried, the door opened enough for her to squeeze through. She stumbled and fell to the hard floor with a grunt.

Close the door. Get up and close it. Now.

As she obeyed the command in her head, she heard something behind her. With the wail of the wind muted by the closed door, she listened. There it was again. The unmistakable huff of a horse and the stomp of its hoof. A cry of relief escaped her lips as she felt her way across the barn. If there was a horse, there must be a person nearby as well.

Her hand hit the railing of a stall. She raised her arms. "Are you there?"

In answer, the horse huffed again.

She laughed, the sound slightly hysterical. Then her legs gave way, and she crumpled to the floor, the darkness overwhelming her.

FIFTEEN

J eremiah was shucking off his shirt, ready to crawl into bed for the night, when something stopped him. An odd need to check on the horse one last time. A foolish thought, he told himself. The buckskin had food and water, and it was protected from the wind and cold.

And yet the tug to return to the barn wouldn't leave him.

Disgusted with himself—the fire in the stove had warmed him clean through and he was ready for sleep—he pulled on coat and hat and headed outside once again.

The wind wasn't as strong as before, and in the lamplight, he could see the snowfall had lessened. Still, he ran his gloved hand along the rope to guide his way to the barn. Once there he had to clean snow away from the ground before he could pull the door open.

The gelding snorted as Jeremiah entered, then tossed its head and turned in a restless circle. The animal appeared more disturbed now than when the storm had been at its worst.

"What is it, fella?" He moved toward the stall. "Easy there."

Another step and he would have kicked the bundle on the floor.

"What—?" He lowered the lantern. It wasn't a bundle. It was a body. A body wrapped in something gray. A gray cloak. Alarm shivered through him as he squatted. "Sarah?"

He pulled off a glove and held his fingers to her forehead. She felt cold to his touch. Lifeless.

"Sarah," he said again, louder this time. He patted her cheek. "Wake up."

A soft moan escaped her.

Thank God.

"Sarah, you need to help me. You've got to stand. We've got to get you into the house so we can get you warm. Do you hear me?" He rose and hung the lantern on a nail. "Come on, Sarah. Let's get you to your feet."

She moaned again. When her eyes opened at last, they didn't focus.

Jeremiah pulled her to a standing position. Before he could step closer, she started to collapse. Rather than let her fall, he swept her feet off the ground. Pain shot up his leg from the old wound in his thigh. He ignored it.

With the rope guide brushing his right hip, he carried her to the house, his heart racing. Once inside, he took her to the stove and placed her on the floor, as close to the heat as he could safely put her.

"Sarah?" He pushed the fur-lined hood away from her face.

Snow melted, dripping onto the wood floor, forming little puddles all around her. He touched her cheek again. Her face was pale, her lips blue. As he loosened her cloak, he felt that her clothes were soaked through. Despite the heat from the stove, she shivered.

"You need to wake up. You need to get out of those wet things."

He took one of her hands and rubbed it between his. What if she had frostbite? What if she lost fingers or toes or even a whole limb? What if she died?

"Sarah!" Her name came out a shout, but there was no sign that she registered it.

He closed his eyes. He wouldn't let her die. He wouldn't see another woman in his care pass from this world to the next.

He got up and went in search of dry clothes and as many blankets as he could find.

SARAH HURT. SHE HURT ALL OVER. NEEDLES POKED INTO HER SKIN, into her joints.

A voice tried to penetrate the pain and the cold. A voice that offered comfort. She wanted to reach for it, but she hadn't the strength. Couldn't even open her eyes.

She was sinking. Sinking into a black, bottomless pit. And she didn't care.

Relief. She wanted relief.

SEVERAL TIMES DURING THE LONG NIGHT THAT FOLLOWED, JEREMIAH added wood to the stove, keeping the fire hot and the house as warm as possible. Hourly, he unwrapped Sarah's feet and briskly rubbed them between his hands, hoping to make the blood flow more freely. He repeated the action with her hands, drawing close to blow warm air onto her fingers. When he finished and Sarah was back within the tight cocoon of blankets, Jeremiah returned to the nearby chair and watched her.

Her lips were not as blue as when he'd carried her from the

barn, but her face still seemed too pale, despite the nearness of the fire.

When he'd removed her wet clothing and replaced it all with his nightshirt, he hadn't allowed his gaze to linger on her slight form. She was an innocent young woman who deserved her privacy. More than that, she was going to marry his brother in a couple of weeks. But once he'd wrapped her in blankets, light from the fire flickering across her face, there could be no harm in looking, in watching her sleep, in praying for her to recover.

"Sarah," he whispered, "keep fighting. There's a whole lot more you need to see and do. You can make it."

God, help her make it through the night.

SARAH DREAMED OF ANGELS WITH FLOWING WHITE GOWNS AND enormous ivory wings. She dreamed they swept down from the heavens and carried her out of the cold and into a place of warmth. A wonderful warmth. At last. Warmth as she'd never felt before.

"That's it. Time to open your eyes. Come on. Open them."

She fought with her eyelids, trying to force them to obey. When at last they did, she saw nothing but a blur of shadow and light, and she allowed her eyes to drift closed again.

"Come on, Sarah. Look at me."

She drew in a breath, concentrating, and opened her eyes again. This time she saw that someone was near. Seated beside her. Bending over her.

Jeremiah?

She blinked.

He smiled.

Her heart reacted.

Why was Jeremiah in her bedroom?

His hand slipped beneath her head and neck. "Take a sip of water. Can you?" He placed a cup to her lips. "That's it. Just a few sips."

She swallowed the water. "What...?" But more words wouldn't form in her mind, and she closed her eyes again.

When she opened them next, the room seemed a little brighter. Enough that she could tell she wasn't in her bedroom at home. If not there, where? She tried to move her arms, wanting to sit up, but she couldn't move them. They were bound to her side. Panic sluiced through her as she struggled to free herself.

"Whoa, there." Once again, Jeremiah's face appeared above her. "It's okay."

"I can't...I can't move."

"Sure you can. You're just wrapped tight in those blankets to keep you warm."

She released a breath. "Where am I? What happened?"

"I hoped you could tell me." He tugged at the blankets, loosening their hold on her. "I found you in the barn, half frozen to death."

"The barn." It all began to come to her then. The fall from the wagon bed. The wind and the cold. The blinding snow. The dark. "Michael and Rosalie." She breathed out their names. "The children."

Jeremiah frowned. "Were they hurt?"

"I don't know. I don't think so. I helped the children from the wagon bed." She remembered pushing Benjamin toward his mother. Had Rosalie caught him? Was the boy safe? Were they all safe? "Then I...I was tossed over the side, and I fell down the mountain. When I was able, I began walking, hoping I would find shelter. Somehow...somehow I stumbled upon your barn."

"Thank God for that." He rose and went to the window. "It's still snowing, but not as bad as last night. They'll send a search party as soon as they can. If the Randolphs made it back to town yesterday, they'll be looking for you. If not..." He let the sentence drift into silence.

"Grandpa." She started to struggle against the blankets again, then realized she wore nothing but a nightshirt. Surprised, she looked around and caught her breath. Someone had made a bed of blankets for her beside the wood stove. Jeremiah? More blankets were stacked on top of her. But where were her clothes? She didn't remember anything after managing to pry open the door to the barn. What on earth—?

"Be still, Sarah. You aren't fit to go anywhere."

"But Michael and Rosalie. I need to know what happened to them and the children. And Grandpa will be worried. Grandpa and Tom need to know what happened. I must tell them."

Jeremiah returned and squatted by her bed on the floor, placing a hand on her shoulder. "There's nothing you can do right now. You need to stay warm. I don't think you've suffered frostbite, but for now, you need to stay by this fire."

"My clothes," she whispered.

A flicker of something crossed his face. "Your clothes are on the other side of the stove. Probably dry by now. Maybe not your boots yet, but the rest."

"How did I—?" She broke off, unable to ask the question.

He looked away. "I had to get you out of those wet things."

She may have nearly frozen to death yesterday, but heat seared through her now. Jeremiah had undressed her.

"There was nothing...untoward." The words sounded clipped, almost insulted.

"No. Of course. I never thought—"

"I only did what I had to do to get you warm and dry." He

rose. "I need to check on the horse. When I come back, I'll fix you something to eat."

"Jeremiah." She lifted a hand toward him, although it took almost more strength than she possessed. "Wait."

He took her hand and squatted beside her again.

"Thank you."

He nodded as he squeezed her fingers, and the way he looked at her caused something strange to coil on her insides.

"I won't be long." He stood. "Close your eyes and rest."

CHAPTER
SIXTEEN

J eremiah trudged through the snow on the way to the barn. He'd needed distance between himself and the beautiful woman lying on the floor near the old wood stove. He'd seen the alarm in her eyes when she'd realized he was the one who'd disrobed her. He'd barely looked at her when he'd removed her wet clothing. He'd thought of little other than trying to save her life. That was all that had mattered to him. But he was no saint nor was he blind. He knew what lay beneath those blankets and the nightshirt. And now that Sarah was awake, it would be better if he made himself absent for a time.

Because what he'd wanted to do, after she'd reached for his hand and thanked him, was to lean down and kiss her. Stopping himself from doing exactly that had been almost impossible. But he'd managed to rise, put on his hat and coat, and leave. And if he was smart, he'd stay in the barn until he got control of his wayward thoughts. Until he remembered that Sarah could never be anything more to him than a sister-in-law.

After clearing the ground once again so the barn door could open, he went inside, breathing in the scent of hay and horse. His breath pooled in front of his face. The temperature was dropping. He didn't like the idea of trying to get Sarah back to Boulder Creek in weather like this. She needed to be kept warm. Should he leave her alone and make the trek on horseback by himself? With the heavy drifts, it could take a lot longer to get there and back, even if the return trip was with a sleigh. He didn't doubt that a search party—or several of them —would start out from town as soon as the snowstorm blew over. Probably before then. Maybe a search was already in process.

The buckskin thrust his head over the stall railing and nickered.

"Yeah, you don't want to go out in this either. But we'll have to eventually." He dropped hay into the feed bin.

"Jeremiah. Wait." Sarah's words echoed in his head. *"Thank you."* They echoed in his heart.

Something came alive inside him. Hope?

"Hello in the house!"

The voice from outside startled him. He moved to the barn door and opened it. Through the falling snow he saw a number of men on horseback and two horses pulling a sleigh. One man had dismounted already and was almost to the door of the house.

"I'm in the barn," he called.

The man near his front door was a stranger to him, but as Jeremiah stepped outside, he recognized Tom McNeal and George Blake among the riders.

"Jeremiah," Tom called, a frightened note in his voice, "we're looking for Sarah. She got lost in the blizzard yesterday. Will you join us?"

"Are the Randolphs okay?" He knew the answer, based on Tom's choice of words, but asked it anyway.

"Yes, but how did—?"

"Sarah's okay too. She's inside." He motioned toward the front door.

In an instant, Tom dismounted. The man already at the door reached out and opened it so Tom could barrel through. Jeremiah crossed the yard with quick strides. When he entered the house, he watched Tom kneel beside his sister.

"Tom?" She stared up at him with a disbelieving gaze.

Before Jeremiah could close the door, other men entered behind him.

Tom looked from Sarah to Jeremiah.

"I found her in the barn last night," Jeremiah said, "froze half to death."

Sarah touched her brother's arm. "Rosalie? The children? Michael?"

"They're all fine," Tom answered. "They made it back to town. Not sure how they made it, as bad as it was. It was all I could do to keep Grandpa from looking for you before morning."

"Jeremiah...saved me."

When Tom looked up again, Jeremiah shook his head. Saving her seemed too strong of praise, but when she turned her gaze in his direction, her blue eyes made him feel like a hero. Then her gaze shifted behind him. He saw the way she clutched the blankets and pulled them to her throat. Immediately he felt her discomfort at her state of undress beneath the blankets.

He faced the men from the search party. "I've got coffee on the stove in the kitchen. Help yourselves. The pot's full." He turned toward Tom again. "I'll heat stones to help keep her warm on the trip back to town." He motioned with his head toward the bedroom. Thankfully, Tom understood.

Jeremiah followed the men into the kitchen area, pointing to cups for the coffee as well as a sugar bowl. When he glanced behind him, Tom, Sarah, and her clothes had disappeared from the living room.

———

TOM BURIED SARAH BENEATH FURS AND BLANKETS IN THE WAGON BED. Warm stones heated her feet and both of her sides. With the driver on the seat, reins in hand, her brother climbed into the wagon beside her.

"Where's Jeremiah?" she asked. "I...I need to thank him for what he did."

"He'll be into town later. Said he wants to wait until the fire burns down in the stove." He reached beneath the blankets to take her hand. "He'll come to check on you. I'm sure of that."

It took effort to focus her eyes on her brother. Too much effort. Her eyelids drifted closed, and she allowed herself to slip into darkness once again.

When she awoke, the snow had stopped falling. From her prone position, she recognized the tall copse of trees near the western entrance into town as the wagon slid beneath the bare and frozen limbs.

"Hey. There you are." Tom's face appeared above her.

She smiled. At least she tried to smile. "Are we almost home?"

"Yes, we are. Warm enough?"

"I think so." She wiggled her fingers and toes. "I slept the whole way."

"Sleep's good for the body when you're recovering from trauma."

She closed her eyes. "You sound like a doctor already."

Tom chuckled. "Thanks."

A couple of men called goodbye, and Tom returned thanks for their help. The sleigh made a turn and not long after came to a halt.

A heartbeat later, Grandpa's voice rang out. "Did you find her?"

"She's here, Grandpa," Tom answered. "She'll be okay."

Sarah struggled to sit up. Her brother put a hand on her shoulder and held her down with a light touch.

"Sarah." Grandpa sounded closer now. "Sarah, are you all right?"

Tom relented and helped her sit up. Her gaze found her grandfather at the side of the wagon.

"Oh, my girl. My girl. What a fright we had."

"Jeremiah found me."

Tom said, "There's a little more to the story than that." He eased her toward the back of the wagon. "She walked out of the mountains herself, Grandpa. In the blizzard. Somehow she made it through the storm to the farm." Her brother hopped to the ground, then turned and reached for her. "A miracle. And another miracle that Jeremiah went out to the barn when he did. If he'd gone earlier or not at all..." His voice drifted into silence.

"Thank the good Lord," Grandpa whispered.

Tom repeated his thanks to the man driving the wagon before carrying Sarah into the house and up the stairs to her room. Her grandfather followed behind. Tom barely had time to set Sarah on the bed before Rosalie Randolph appeared in the doorway.

"Thank God." Rosalie rushed forward, sat beside Sarah, and hugged her. "I was watching from the window in the hotel, praying for your return. We were so worried. Michael looked for you but—" Her voice broke.

"I'm all right, Rosalie. Is Benjamin safe? And Sophia? I was afraid—"

"They're both fine. We're all fine. It's you we are worried about."

"I'm all right," she repeated. "Just tired."

Her friend stood again. "Leave us alone, gentlemen, and I'll get her into bed."

"I'll send for Doc," Grandpa said as he and Tom backed out of the room.

As Rosalie helped Sarah remove her clothes, she told her about Michael's frantic search for Sarah as the storm worsened, their frightening journey back to Boulder Creek, and the long wait for the blizzard to blow itself out. "Michael blames himself for the accident. He wanted to go with the search party this morning, but Doc wouldn't let him."

"Why not?" Clad in a fresh nightgown, Sarah sank onto the edge of the bed again.

"I didn't say that part, did I?" Rosalie eased Sarah back on the pillows and pulled the blanket and top quilt over her. "He fell and broke his arm when he was trying to find you."

"Oh, no."

"Doc says it isn't anything to worry about. If Michael's careful, it should heal in a matter of weeks." She took hold of Sarah's hand. "He's so sorry. He called and called your name. We all did. He went as far down the mountain as he dared. But he couldn't find you. The world had turned completely white by then."

"It wasn't Michael's fault. And he had to take care of all of you."

Rosalie nodded. "We were lost ourselves. Getting down to the valley was terrifying. Michael thought we would find shelter at the Rocking D or one of the farms on the way, but we passed right by them in the storm. Never saw a single building until we reached Boulder Creek. And that was a miracle. We could have been going north instead of east." Tears streaked her friend's cheeks.

"Rosalie, stop." She squeezed her friend's hand. "It was an accident. No one is at fault, and God took care of me. I made it to safety." Jeremiah's concerned face appeared in her memory. How she wished he was with her still. His presence had been...calming.

Except when it had been disturbing.

"All is well," she added in a whisper.

"You're very gracious." Rosalie wiped her eyes with her fingertips before standing. "I'd better let your grandfather and brother into the room again. They need reassurance that you're well."

CHAPTER
SEVENTEEN

On Sunday morning, with her brother and grandfather attending church, Sarah grew restless in the quiet of the empty house. The doctor had ordered her to stay in bed on Saturday, tucked in with warming stones by her hands and feet. Tom had brought her lunch and supper on a tray the previous day and had repeated the act for breakfast that morning.

"But I'm not eating Sunday dinner in bed," she muttered as she pushed aside the blanket and quilt that covered her.

Her body felt bruised from her long tumble down the mountain two days before, but nothing was broken, unlike Michael's arm. Sleep had restored much of her strength, and if anyone came to see her today, she didn't want to be found in bed.

Anyone. Meaning Jeremiah.

Despite Tom's assurance that Jeremiah would come to see her when he returned to Boulder Creek, he hadn't come. Neither had Warren, but that was because he'd stayed a second night in Boise City.

She frowned.

Warren had been informed of the accident by telegram, but he hadn't hurried back on the next train. His business had been more pressing than the health of his fiancée. Strangely, that knowledge didn't hurt her feelings. It was the way Warren was and had always been. And since she intended to break the engagement the next time they were alone together, it didn't matter that he was more concerned with his possible business merger in Boise. In fact, it gave her courage to do what she needed to do.

She washed quickly and dressed in a favorite yellow gown, refusing to admit that the effort left her exhausted. After tying her hair with a ribbon at the nape, she made her way downstairs, fixed herself a cup of tea, and settled on the sofa near the fireplace. She'd taken only a few sips from the cup when she heard the front door open.

Tom was saying something to Grandpa as the two men entered the parlor, but he stopped abruptly when he saw her. "Sarah, what are you doing downstairs?"

"I'm enjoying a cup of tea."

"You were told to stay in bed."

"I was told to stay in bed yesterday. I'm much better today."

Tom stepped toward her, and it was only then that she saw Jeremiah behind him. Her heart stuttered. Seeing him made her remember—more fully than before—how he'd cared for her the night of the storm.

"It's good to see you feeling better," he said. How tender his voice was, how tender his gaze.

"Thank you." A flush warmed her cheeks.

Grandpa said, "We asked Jeremiah to join us for dinner. Several of our neighbors gave us food the women had prepared for the Christmas social."

"The social." She glanced up. "I'd forgotten it."

"It was postponed because of the storm," Tom offered. "So folks had plenty of leftovers to share."

Sarah started to rise.

Grandpa stopped her. "No. You stay there. Tom and I will manage." He motioned to a chair. "Jeremiah, have a seat."

Jeremiah waited until the other two men left the parlor, then he sat. His gaze went to the fireplace for a time but eventually returned to Sarah. "You do look much improved."

"I am. *Much* improved." She gave a brief smile. "A little tired still."

"And no frostbite?"

"No frostbite. Doc Varney said you took good care of me." Again she felt heat creep up her neck.

"I tried my best. I'm thankful I was at the farm when the blizzard hit."

"So am I."

A smile tipped the corners of his mouth. Her heart responded with another skip of a beat, and she wished he could go on smiling at her forever.

A knock on the front door intruded on the thought.

"Ah, Warren." Grandpa's voice reached her from the entry hall. "You're back. Come in. Come in."

Jeremiah's smile vanished in an instant, and Sarah's stomach knotted.

"How is she?"

"See for yourself. She's in the parlor."

Warren entered the room. He saw Sarah first and nodded. Then he noticed Jeremiah, and his expression hardened. "I came as soon as I could." His gaze swung back to Sarah.

That wasn't true. He could have returned yesterday. But she didn't say so.

Warren crossed the room and brushed a kiss against the cheek she turned to him.

Today. I must tell him today.

Warren faced his brother. "I hear you found her. They're making you out to be a hero."

"I'm not a hero. It was God's doing that she made her way to the farm."

It saddened Sarah, that Jeremiah felt the need to minimize his part in her rescue, especially to Warren.

Tell him now.

She set the teacup aside and pushed herself up from the sofa. "Warren, could we speak privately?"

He looked at her with surprise.

"Please. We can use Grandpa's study."

"If you insist."

She led the way out of the parlor, silently praying for the right words to say.

JEREMIAH'S CHEST HURT, AN ACHE THAT MADE HIM WANT TO BOLT from the house. No, not just from this house. It made him want to bolt from Boulder Creek.

He stayed put. He was done running away. For too many years, he'd run from pain, from life, from friends, from love. No more. Not even when his heart pulled him toward the wrong woman. And Sarah was definitely the wrong woman.

Hank McNeal reentered the parlor, his gaze sweeping the room.

Jeremiah pointed toward the study. "They wanted a minute alone."

"Ah."

"Can I help with anything? The dinner, I mean."

"No, son. Tom's setting the food on the table now. But it's nothing fancy. Won't mind waiting for those two." The older man smiled, but the expression was mingled with a look of concern.

Warren's voice reached them through the closed door, muffled but raised. He didn't sound happy. Were they having a lovers' tiff on the heels of Sarah's narrow escape from a frozen grave? His brother couldn't be that big of a fool, could he?

As if in answer, the door to the study flew open and Warren came out. He stopped and pointed a finger. "This is your fault!"

Jeremiah stood. "What is?"

"I don't know what you did, but I know you did something."

He thought of Sarah, bathed in light from the flickering fire, so cold and fragile. He'd wanted to hold her to him and never let go. He'd wanted to cradle her in his arms. He'd done only what was necessary to help her and no more. But he'd *wanted* more. How had this happened? How had he let her mean more to him than she should?

He lifted a hand. "Warren, look—"

His brother took a wild swing. Jeremiah leaned back in time, and Warren's fist flew past him without making contact.

Hank stepped toward them. "Warren, stop." He sounded every inch the sheriff.

Warren swore beneath his breath. He looked from Hank to Jeremiah, then swiveled toward the entry hall. Tom moved into view a moment before Warren pushed past him, slamming the door as he left the house.

Silence fell over the parlor.

Finally, Tom asked, "What's wrong with him?"

"It's because of me."

The three men turned to see Sarah standing in the doorway to the study.

Looking almost as pale and lifeless as she had on Friday night, Sarah moved to the sofa.

"My girl." Hank crossed the room to sit next to her. "What is it? What's happened?"

"I told Warren I couldn't marry him."

The breath caught in Jeremiah's chest as a mixture of emotions swept through him. Emotions he couldn't define. Or perhaps he was afraid to define them.

"The wedding is off," Sarah added softly.

CHAPTER

EIGHTEEN

I'm going to the mercantile," Sarah announced on Thursday.

She gave her grandfather and brother a look that said she would brook no argument. They had hovered over her for days. She wasn't sure which caused them the most concern—her accident in the blizzard or her decision not to marry Warren.

"I am well." She looked from Grandpa to Tom and back again. "And we are in need of supplies."

"I can—" Grandpa began, but he wisely closed his mouth.

She pulled on her cloak. "I must do some baking now that the Christmas social has been rescheduled."

Grandpa and Tom exchanged a look, but Sarah chose to ignore them. She needed fresh air.

Outside, the sky was a cloudless blue. The snow that had blanketed the valley the previous week remained deep, and high drifts rose against the sides of houses and other buildings. It would be a white Christmas for sure.

Hard to believe Christmas was only three days away. And three days after that would be her birthday.

She stopped walking.

If I hadn't broken my engagement, my wedding would be one week from today.

She waited to see if the thought brought disappointment. It didn't. The only thing she regretted was that she'd agreed to marry Warren in the first place. It had been wrong of her. She hadn't loved him, and she was quite certain he'd never loved her. He'd been angered by her decision, but he hadn't been hurt. Only his pride had been wounded.

And he blamed Jeremiah.

She continued walking down North Street until the jail came into view. Then she stopped again.

Was Jeremiah sitting at the desk in the sheriff's office now? Had another woman taken him lunch each day this week or had he eaten at Zoe's or the hotel for every meal? And why hadn't he come to supper last night? It had been agreed that he should dine at the McNeal house on Wednesdays. Of course, that had been when she was engaged to his brother.

Her pulse stuttered as she remembered him leaning over her. She'd been scarcely conscious, yet that image was burned into her memory.

In that moment, she'd wanted him to kiss her.

Heart racing, she hurried across Main Street, then followed the boardwalk to the mercantile. The chime of a small bell announced her arrival.

"Sarah!" Leslie came from behind the counter, brushing her hands on her apron. "Oh, it's good to see you out and about."

Sarah smiled. "Thank you."

"Everyone thinks it's a miracle that you survived."

"Yes."

"Thank God Mr. West found you when he did."

She nodded, and again the memory of him, the firelight flickering across his face, flashed in her mind.

Leslie lowered her voice. "We were all very sorry to hear about you and Warren." Curiosity filled her eyes.

She knew what the other woman wanted to ask: *Why? What went wrong?* Sarah gave her head a small shake as she produced a written list of the supplies she wanted to buy. "We need a few things." She handed the slip of paper to Leslie.

"Of course. Of course."

The door opened again, and two older women—Ethel Bonnell and Cara O'Rourke—entered the store. When they saw Sarah, Ethel gave a curt nod before pulling Cara toward a corner. Once there, they began to whisper. Sarah didn't have to hear their words to know they gossiped about her. But what were they saying?

Tom had taken the news of the broken engagement to the reverend as well as to Madeline Gaunt at the dress shop. Her brother wouldn't have said anything other than the wedding was off, which meant the gossips in town needed to manufacture their own reasons.

Or had Warren said something to someone? She remembered the anger in his voice as he'd shouted that Sarah's decision was Jeremiah's fault. She remembered the wild swing of his fist. But it wasn't Jeremiah's fault. Jeremiah had done nothing wrong. Not ever. Not a wrong word. Not a wrong look. Not a wrong action.

All he did was win my heart.

JEREMIAH RUBBED THE CREASES IN HIS FOREHEAD WITH THE FINGERS OF one hand. A headache made it difficult to concentrate on the words in the report from the sheriff in Ada County.

He left his chair and went to pour himself another cup of coffee. But after a sip, he knew he needed something to eat. He'd skipped breakfast, and hunger gnawed at his stomach. Perhaps that was the reason for the throbbing in his head.

But what ailed him had nothing to do with lack of food, and he knew it. Over the past few days, he'd become aware of odd looks and whispered conversations when people saw him. And he'd caught just enough words, here and there, to know a few less-kindly people suspected more had happened in his house on the night of the blizzard than the rescue of a young woman—a suspicion they no doubt believed was confirmed by the broken engagement of Sarah McNeal to Warren West.

Frowning, Jeremiah left the office and strode down the boardwalk that had been cleared of snow.

He hadn't seen either Sarah or Warren since Sunday. He'd watched for them when making his usual rounds, but he hadn't ventured near either of their doors. With the weather as cold as it was, he supposed it was no surprise that they—like most others in town—remained inside.

He stopped and glanced up the street toward the McNeal home. Had Sarah's health taken a turn for the worse? That could be a reason he hadn't seen her in these last few days before Christmas. But surely he would have heard if she was ill. He remembered how pale she'd looked after Warren stormed out of the house. She'd said the decision not to marry had been hers. Was that true?

"Deputy West," a familiar voice called to him.

Jeremiah turned to see Michael Randolph crossing the street, his right arm in a sling.

"Headed to Zoe's?" Michael asked.

"Yes." Jeremiah moved forward again.

Michael fell into step with him. "Mind if I join you?"

"At Zoe's? Don't you eat at the hotel?"

"Most days, but I like a change every now and then."

"Then I'll welcome your company."

"The Christmas social is on for Saturday," Michael said, "weather permitting. You'll be there?"

"I reckon."

"Rosalie thought they should cancel, what with all the snow and Saturday being Christmas Eve, but she was overruled. Folks look forward to the social. Guess it just wouldn't feel like the Christmas season in Boulder Creek without it." Michael cleared his throat. "And there are some who want to see if Sarah and Warren show up. Separately or together."

Jeremiah stopped. "People should leave the two of them be."

"I suppose the gossips need to flap their jaws to keep warm." Michael shrugged. "It has been a bitter cold December."

Jeremiah grunted in response to the joke, then moved toward the entrance to Zoe's Restaurant. Inside, the two men had plenty of tables to choose from. Few people, it seemed, had ventured out today. They sat at a table near the far wall. Jeremiah glanced at the menu on the chalkboard by the front door, and his stomach growled.

Michael chuckled. "Sounds like you're ready for lunch."

Before Zoe or another waitress could come to take their order, the door opened again, this time admitting Rosalie, followed by Sarah.

Rosalie smiled when she saw them. "This is a surprise." She gave a nod to Jeremiah, then returned her gaze to her husband. "Should Chef Petit be concerned that we found you here?"

"No." Michael lowered his voice. "It doesn't hurt to check out the competition on occasion. What's your excuse?" He motioned to the empty chairs at the table in wordless invitation.

"I ran into Sarah at the mercantile, and we decided to enjoy lunch together. You know I wouldn't get a moment's peace if we ate at the hotel."

Michael chuckled, adoration in his eyes as he told his wife, "I'll grant you that."

Jeremiah kept his eyes on the married couple for as long as possible, but he couldn't help glancing at Sarah as she settled onto the chair to his left, her own gaze averted from him. When he'd left the sheriff's office, this had been the last encounter he'd expected to have—as well as the one he'd wanted most. But what should he say to her? How should he act? He'd heard the gossip. Had she?

"We aren't intruding, are we?" Rosalie removed her gloves.

"No," Michael answered. "Who would turn away such charming company?"

Zoe Paddock appeared out of the kitchen, welcoming each of them with a nod. "Mr. and Mrs. Randolph. Miss McNeal. Deputy West." She kept her gaze on Jeremiah. "What can I get for you?"

He glanced at the menu a second time. "Have you got any of the roast beef left?"

"I do."

"Then that's what I'll have."

"And for you, Miss McNeal?"

As the proprietress looked at Sarah, Jeremiah did the same. Although her complexion remained pale and her cheeks were without color, she didn't look sick so much as unhappy. Did she regret her broken engagement to Warren? And if so, could he help?

Appetite gone, his gut told him this would be an uncomfortable meal.

CHAPTER
NINETEEN

S arah had cried herself to sleep every night for the past week, but when she awakened Friday morning, she determined not to feel sorry for herself a moment longer. She had been right to call off the wedding. She hadn't loved Warren, and whether he admitted it or not, he hadn't loved her. She'd been wrong—and had told him so in her grandfather's study —to accept his proposal. She'd done him a favor by ending the engagement. It would have been tragic for them both if they'd gone through with the wedding.

Pushing her hair away from her face, she sat on the side of the bed and pulled a blanket around her shoulders against the morning chill. Eyes closed, she said a prayer for the day ahead. Then she rose. As she hurriedly washed and dressed, her thoughts drifted to Jeremiah—as they'd done so often throughout the week. She recalled the tension that had stretched between them at the restaurant the previous day. She knew *her* reasons for feeling awkward in his presence. What had been his?

"What a mess I've made of things."

Ready for the day, she left her room. Downstairs, she discovered that someone had already added fuel to the fire in the kitchen stove. The scent of coffee filled the air.

"Grandpa?"

No answer.

"Tom?"

Again, only silence.

She glanced out the window. The world looked gray in these minutes before sunrise. Gray, reflective of her mood. But no, she was done with dark thoughts. She had a new life to build for herself. She didn't know what her future held. Perhaps the stuff of her dreams would never come true, but that didn't mean she wouldn't find happiness.

Again, Jeremiah invaded her thoughts.

If only—

"Morning, sis." Tom stepped into the kitchen, a cup in hand. He refilled it with coffee before leaning against the counter. "You look more yourself this morning."

"Do I?"

He nodded. "A bit of color in your cheeks. That's a good sign."

"Thank you, Dr. McNeal."

"You're welcome. And what have you planned for the day?"

"I'm baking cookies for the social."

"May I help?"

"If you want."

"I get to lick the bowl. Right?"

A memory of her and Tom—when they were perhaps eight and five—flashed in her mind. The two of them in this kitchen with Grandma. The laughter. The jostling for the spoon and bowl to lick the last of the cookie dough.

The sweet remembrance faded as she imagined Jeremiah and Warren as children. No mother or grandmother making cookies in the kitchen. No shared laughter. Had they ever been close, the two of them? It was doubtful, and she felt sorry for them. Whatever bitter seed had been planted in Warren's heart—no matter the cause—it had only increased since Jeremiah's return.

"What's wrong?" Tom asked softly.

She blinked, then shook her head. "Nothing. I just think I'm blessed to have you as my brother."

"Because I like cookie dough?"

"No." She slapped his arm with a towel. "Because you're you."

"Thanks, I guess." He set down the cup, then pushed off the counter and went to a hook on the wall where he selected the top apron. He tied it around his waist. "Ready when you are."

Yes, it was going to be a brighter day. No more gray skies for her.

Jeremiah closed the cell door. "It's way too early in the day for this."

Bart Haskell collapsed onto the cot with a groan and rolled onto his side, his back toward Jeremiah.

"You're lucky I found you, Bart. You would've frozen to death if you'd been outside all day."

A snore reverberated in the small space.

With a shake of his head, Jeremiah returned to the front office. Hank had warned him that letting a man sleep off too much drink would not be uncommon in Boulder Creek. The Pony Saloon did a brisk business. But putting a man in the cell at one in the afternoon was unusual. Especially since he'd found the fellow sitting in the snow between two buildings.

And with the temperature lingering in the single digits, Bart might have never awakened again if he'd gone undiscovered.

Jeremiah rubbed the back of his neck. Maybe he'd better have Doc take a look at the prisoner. Bart wouldn't be sober enough to say if he was in pain. One thing for certain: Jeremiah didn't intend to rub Bart's hands and feet the way he had Sarah's.

Sarah.

His thoughts went to her constantly. He remembered her, pale and helpless, on the floor in front of the stove in the West farmhouse. He remembered her, ashen after her encounter with Warren on Sunday. He remembered her as she'd been yesterday, sadness lingering on her delicate features.

There was no denying his attraction to her, but he wouldn't allow himself to act on it. He'd lived alone ever since Marta's death. He would continue that way. He would serve this town as its deputy. He would work his land. It was a good enough life. It had to be enough.

He pictured the sweetness of Sarah's smile and the gentleness in the blue of her eyes. He remembered her in this office, at church, in the dining room of her home. Sarah McNeal deserved to be happy. She deserved to be loved. He couldn't give her the things that would make her happy, but somewhere out there was the right man for her. If not Warren, someone else. He hoped she would find him soon. And whoever that special someone was, he hoped to heaven that man would take her away from Boulder Creek, because he couldn't bear to think of her so close while belonging to another.

Shaking his head, trying to free himself from such thoughts, he poured the last dregs of coffee from the pot on the stove. He took a sip, then wrinkled his nose in distaste. It was bitter beyond what he could tolerate.

The door opened, letting in a blast of cold air along with the sheriff.

Jeremiah moved the pot to the back of the stove and set the cup of remaining coffee on the shelf.

"Afternoon." Hank stomped snow off his boots before closing the door.

"Sir."

He motioned toward the pot. "Any coffee left?"

"No, sir. Not a drop."

"Just as well." The sheriff moved to a chair and sat on it with a sigh. "Anything happening I should know about?"

"No, sir." Jeremiah went to the chair behind the desk. "Bart Haskell's sleeping off the drink in a cell."

"Early for that."

"That's what I thought." He sat, wondering what had brought the older man to the office.

As if in answer to the unspoken question, Hank said, "I needed to get out of the house. Sarah and Tom are baking for tomorrow's social."

"Tom's baking?"

"My wife thought it was good for a boy to learn to fend for himself."

"True enough."

"I suppose it is, but those two are making a horrible racket."

"I never thought baking a noisy affair."

Hank chuckled. "Not usually. But they're swapping stories from when they were little. Then they start laughing and pushing and shoving, just like back then. You should see them. Both covered in flour and whatnot."

Jeremiah would like to see Sarah laughing and covered in flour and whatnot. Far better than the sad expression she'd worn the previous day.

Again, Hank seemed to speak to Jeremiah's thoughts. "It does me good, seeing her spirits improve. I've been concerned." He ran fingers through his thinning hair. "She won't talk about what happened between her and Warren. Do you know?"

"No, sir. Haven't seen my brother since he took that swing at me. And, in case I need to say it, I don't know why he blames me. There's nothing between me and your granddaughter. She's been kind to me. Like a sister. Nothing more."

The words were true, yet they felt like a lie on his tongue. Because his heart yearned for so much more.

TWENTY

On Saturday, folks came to the Christmas social from miles around, most of them arriving in sleighs, a few on horseback. The Mason barn, located on the far edge of town, had been swept clean. Potbellied stoves in two corners took some of the chill from the building, but most people kept their coats on. Makeshift tables lined one wall. Two hours before, they'd been laden with food, but most of the bowls and platters had been emptied by the time the musicians picked up fiddle, guitar, and mouth organ and began to play.

"Would you care to dance, Miss McNeal?"

Sarah shook her head at the lanky Rocking D cowboy. "I'm sorry, Mr. Chase. I'm not dancing today."

He gave her a nod and moved off.

"You should've accepted," Leslie Blake said.

"There's enough gossip without that."

Leslie touched Sarah's arm, her expression sobering. "I'm sorry about the talk." She looked across the barn to where Warren stood with a few townsmen. "It'll die down. Something new'll come along, and folks will forget that you and Warren planned to marry."

Sarah hoped that was true. She'd done the right thing, ending her engagement. Of that she was sure. Still, it hurt—the way a few people she'd known her entire life had looked at her today.

Warren chose that moment to turn in her direction. She saw the angry cut of his jaw and felt the resentment, like a blast of heat from the potbellied stove in the nearest corner. Then he strode to the raised stage and lifted his arms. "Could I have your attention?"

The musicians fell silent first, followed by the crowd.

"Thank you. I've got some news I'd like to share with you all."

An ominous feeling seeped through Sarah's veins.

"Some of you have heard I was down in Boise City at the time of the blizzard. You might find it interesting that they had no snow on the ground when I left. The storm missed them completely."

There was a murmur of surprise.

Warren raised his hands again to recall their attention. "For those of you who haven't been down that way in a few years, I can tell you the capital is thriving. It's an exciting place." He grinned. "That's why I've accepted Mr. Kubicki's offer to form a partnership. You've all heard of Kubicki & Company. Well, the name is now Kubicki, West & Company. We'll be making fine, affordable furniture to be shipped everywhere in the country. I'll move to Boise right after the first of the year." His gaze shot to Sarah. "There is certainly nothing to keep me in Boulder Creek."

More eyes turned in her direction.

"I hope to find that Boise is a place where a woman keeps her promises and where a brother doesn't take what isn't his."

Gasps erupted, then the barn went dead silent. Grandpa and Tom bolted to their feet. She reached for her brother's arm. "Don't," she said softly as she rose to stand beside him.

She looked at Warren again, and in that moment, she realized she wasn't angry for what he'd said. He'd wanted to embarrass her, to shame her. He'd wanted members of the community to be on his side rather than hers, and perhaps he would succeed. But she couldn't be angry for that either. All she could do was feel sorry for him. She pitied him. Nothing more.

She knew the instant he comprehended her reaction. His eyes widened, his lips flattened, and he stepped off the platform, pushing his way through the crowd until he reached the door. He didn't look back before disappearing from view.

STANDING NOT FAR FROM THE BARN DOOR, JEREMIAH WAITED A FEW moments before following his brother outside. "Warren!"

Warren whirled around.

Jeremiah quickened his steps. But the look on Warren's face stopped him before he could get too close. No point in putting himself in danger of another fist flying past his jaw.

"Go back inside, Jeremiah."

"I don't want us to part on bad terms."

"That's the only way we can part."

"Why?"

"We've never been on good terms. What does it matter now?"

"It matters. I want things to be right between us."

Warren started walking away. "We don't always get what we want."

Jeremiah followed. "I'm sorry about what happened

between you and Sarah, but it has nothing to do with me. You shouldn't have said what you did back there."

Warren stopped again. "She changed after you came back."

"I don't know about that. I don't remember her from before. She was a child when I left."

"Yes. I was the one who remained in Boulder Creek. I was the one waiting for her to grow up and to agree to marry me."

He searched for something to say, something that could mend whatever was broken between them. He found nothing.

Warren took a step forward. "She would have married me if not for you."

"She's never been anything but kind to me. She's treated me as she does everyone. Whatever you imagine, it isn't true."

"Something happened. Something changed. That's all I know."

Jeremiah turned up the collar of his coat against the cold. "So you're really moving to Boise City."

"Yes. You'll be rid of me in a couple of weeks."

"I never wanted to be rid of you. I hoped we could get to know each other."

Warren grunted, a sound of disbelief.

"I used to be bitter, too." Jeremiah longed to reach out, to somehow break through the invisible wall that separated them. "I carried it like a shield, thinking it would keep me safe, keep me from feeling pain. It didn't work."

"I'm not bitter."

Jeremiah shook his head. "I wish you well in Boise City. I hope you find happiness there. And contentment."

Warren gave another grunt, then strode away.

"I can't fix whatever went wrong if I don't know what it is," he whispered, watching until his brother turned a corner and disappeared from view.

Drawing a deep breath, Jeremiah returned to the barn. He

managed to slip inside without being noticed, thanks to the musicians who played a lively tune. Clapping and stomping and laughter filled the air as dancers whirled about the center of the open room. Unable to keep from it, he looked toward the place Sarah had been a short while before. She was still there, once again seated. Tom wasn't in sight, but Hank had moved to the chair closest to her. The look on the older man's face dared anyone to approach them.

If things were different, Jeremiah might have wished Warren's suspicions were true. If things were different, he might wish that Sarah cared for him. If things were different—

But they weren't. He'd shed himself of bitterness, but there were things he still wouldn't risk. Loving a woman like Sarah was one of them.

Once again, he left the barn, this time for good.

Tears welled in Sarah's eyes, but she blinked them back, hoping no one would see.

It hadn't hurt when Warren tried to malign her reputation with his cutting comments. It hadn't hurt when he stormed out of the barn. But seeing Jeremiah leave again... That hurt for some inexplicable reason.

"Are you all right, my girl?"

"Yes, Grandpa. But I'm a little tired."

"Not surprising. All that baking you did yesterday, and you only just recovered from the accident."

She feigned a smile. She couldn't explain her melancholy. Not to her grandfather. Not to anyone. "Perhaps it is time for me to go home."

Grandpa stood. "I'll take you."

"It isn't that far. You don't need to leave the social on my account."

"Yes, I do. To be honest, I'm feeling a bit done in myself. The music is starting to pound in my head."

They said a few goodbyes as they made their way to the exit and exchanged some wishes for a merry Christmas with those they were unlikely to see at church the following morning. Once outside, Sarah took a deep breath of the crisp air, realizing she hadn't lied to her grandfather. She was tired. And ready to go home.

They walked with care across the snowy terrain. Once away from the barn, the music faded until silence seemed to blanket the town.

As they neared the front door of their house, Grandpa patted Sarah's hand where it rested in the crook of his arm. "That's better, I think."

"What is?"

"Coming home. It's good to be with neighbors, good to have friends, but the coming home is always the best." He opened the door and motioned her in ahead of him.

Sarah removed her coat and hung it on a peg. "You never wanted to leave Boulder Creek, did you?"

"Not from the moment the McNeals first arrived in the territory. It's been a good place for our family." His coat followed Sarah's onto a peg. "And I'm selfish enough that I hope your brother will come back when he's finished his schooling. Doc Varney won't be around forever, and it would be a hard thing to not have a doctor in the valley."

"I feel certain he'll come back. And I'm not going anywhere so you'll have to put up with the both of us for a long time to come."

Her grandfather touched her shoulder. "You aren't sorry, are you?"

"No." She shook her head and smiled at him. "No, I'm not sorry. I don't want to leave Boulder Creek."

"But you used to dream about travel, about visiting places in the East and even in Europe. I remember the way you pretended. Always off in your imagination, going someplace the rest of us couldn't see."

She hooked her arm through his and drew him into the parlor so he could sit by the fire. "Grandpa, I would still love to travel and see the places I've read about. But this is my home. I am *not* sorry to stay right here."

"I wish I could pay for you to have one of those grand adventures." He frowned up at her from his chair. "Seems that Warren is destined to make a name for himself with his new business in Boise City. I'd hoped he could give you what I never could."

"Oh, Grandpa." She knelt and took his hands in hers. "It isn't things or trips or money or prestige that I'd hoped to have if I married Warren. I hoped I would have the kind of love you and Grandma shared. That's all I really wanted. And then I realized Warren could never give me that. That's why I couldn't go through with the wedding."

Grandpa leaned forward and kissed the crown of her head. "You're a wise young woman, Sarah McNeal. A wise young woman."

CHAPTER
TWENTY-ONE

On Christmas morning, Jeremiah stepped into the back row of pews during the opening hymn. While pretending to sing, his gaze swept over the heads of the congregation. It didn't take long to note that Warren wasn't present. Jeremiah hadn't expected him to join the McNeal family, of course, but his brother's absence for the Sunday service saddened him. He knew all too well what it was like to try to avoid God because of personal pain. He hoped it wouldn't take years before Warren let go of bitterness.

With the "Amen" lingering in the air, the congregation took their seats on the wooden pews. Jeremiah glanced across the aisle to find a woman looking at him with a spark of disdain. He supposed she believed his brother's accusation. He nodded in her direction, doing his best not to reveal any emotion, before turning his eyes on the pulpit.

The gossip would end, he told himself. His brother's less than generous words at the social had stirred the talk that started after people first learned of the broken engagement, but it would die down, given time. At least Sarah had family and close friends who would do their best to shield her from snide comments. And if he wanted to help, he would do well to steer clear of her.

The idea cut. He would miss going to Sunday dinners and Wednesday suppers in the McNeal home. He'd been back in Idaho less than a month, but those few meals had made him feel as if he were a part of a family. A real family. Perhaps, in time, he could enjoy their friendship again. But not now.

With a mental shake, he focused his attention on the pastor's sermon, finding comfort in the teaching. When the service ended, he left church without speaking to anyone. Bundled against the cold, he made his usual rounds. Businesses were closed for Christmas, with the exception of the hotel and the saloon.

Finding everything quiet, he entered the main doors of the Randolph Hotel and walked to the restaurant on the east side of the building.

Betty, the waitress, welcomed him with a "Merry Christmas, Deputy West," then led him to a small table against a far wall.

"Thank you, Betty."

"We don't have a menu today," she said with a smile. "Everyone gets the same. Prime rib, sweet potato dressing, and tomatoes in mayonnaise."

He returned her smile, thankful the gossip hadn't turned her against him as it had the woman opposite him in church. "Sounds good."

"I'll bring you a plate straight away."

After she left, voices in the doorway drew his gaze in time to see the Randolph family enter the restaurant.

"Jeremiah." Michael crossed the room and clamped a hand on his shoulder. "You shouldn't eat alone on Christmas Day.

Come join us." He lowered his voice. "Although it will be much noisier at our table."

"I wouldn't want to intrude."

"Nonsense. Come along."

Jeremiah didn't argue. He would prefer being with a family. If not the McNeals, then the Randolphs. He didn't know them well, but it felt as if they were on their way to becoming friends. He stood and grabbed his hat off the empty chair before following Michael to the large round table where Rosalie and the children were getting settled.

"Hope you don't mind," he said to Rosalie.

"Not at all. We planned to invite you to join us, but you left church before we could."

He sat. "I needed to have a look around town before I ate."

"Sheriff McNeal is lucky to have you for his deputy."

Her words warmed him. "And I'm lucky to work under Hank. I've learned a lot in a short period of time."

Michael cleared his throat. "I'll be sorry if your brother's... comments at the social make things difficult for you."

Was that why the Randolphs had asked him to dine with them? The mayor wanted to show support for the town deputy.

An unexpected feeling of sorrow washed over Jeremiah. Sorrow for Warren. Did he have others who'd gathered around him, offering comfort over the broken engagement, lending support to his new business venture? Something in his gut told him the answer was no. Even if someone had tried, Warren would push them away. He would leave Boulder Creek in a trail of anger.

Sarah looked up from the plate before her. "Did I ruin Christmas for you, Grandpa?" Her gaze shifted to her brother. "For both of you?"

"Sarah." Her grandfather drew out her name. "Of course not."

"But we have no guests for Christmas dinner. We usually have so many friends with us." *Jeremiah should be here*, her heart added.

Tom gave a slight shake of his head. "It's better this way. Doc Varney thought you should rest."

"I've done nothing but rest for the past week." That wasn't entirely true, but close enough.

"Your brother's right," Grandpa said gently. "Besides, you saw everyone at the social and some again at church this morning. There was no need for guests for dinner."

"It doesn't feel right." Her words came out almost a whisper.

"You're wrong, my girl. It feels very right. We have celebrated our Lord's birth. We have enjoyed good food. And our family is all present at this table. That is more than some can say."

Her grandfather's words made her feel ashamed for wishing for something more.

Wishing for someone else.

Tears filled her eyes. "Please excuse me." She rose. "I believe the doctor was right. I need to rest."

Tom stood, too. "Shall I fetch Doc?"

"No." She shook her head as she turned from the table. "I'm fine. Only tired. I'll go lie down. A short nap is all I require."

"Don't worry about the dishes," her grandfather said. "Tom and I will clean up."

She wanted to tell Grandpa to leave everything for her, but a few more moments and she would not be able to hide her true distress from these two men. They knew her too well. They loved her too much. She hurried from the dining room.

Upstairs, she sat on the side of her bed, the tears now streaking her cheeks. "What is wrong with me?" Only two days before, she'd decided she would cry no more. And yet, here she was again. "I miss him."

Jeremiah's face appeared in her memory. How was it possible to miss someone she hardly knew? And yet she did miss him.

The lunch at Zoe's a few days earlier had been awkward. She hadn't known what to say to Jeremiah, and she supposed he'd felt much the same. Rosalie and Michael had been left to carry the conversation. But Sarah would give anything to sit across from him right now. To look into his eyes and try to tell him what she felt, even though she wasn't sure what that was.

Was it love?

As a girl, she'd imagined herself falling in love. The man of her dreams had never been clear in her mind, but that hadn't mattered. The rest of her fantasy had been all too enjoyable. However, she was no longer a girl. She was a grown woman. Imagining love wasn't enough. She wanted it for herself. She wanted to love and to be loved.

Could Jeremiah be the man who would win her heart?

Had he won it already?

Yes, he had.

She lay on her side, knees drawn toward her chest.

Grandpa and Tom thought she was tired. She *was* tired. But it had nothing to do with wandering for hours in a blizzard or the cold that tried to steal the life from her. There was a pain in her chest, an ache that wouldn't stop.

Could it be a broken heart?

TWENTY-TWO

J eremiah laid the slip of paper on the mercantile counter. "Here's my list of what I need. And give me a few of those licorice sticks, too, please."

Leslie grinned before pulling the jar off the shelf. "You're as bad as Benjamin Randolph. Every time that boy comes in this store, he heads straight for the candy jars."

Jeremiah could only shrug.

Bells jingled above the door as another customer entered.

Leslie gave a little wave. "Hello, Tom. I'll be with you in a minute."

Jeremiah glanced over his shoulder to watch Sarah's brother approach.

"No hurry," Tom said. "I'm here to pick up Sarah's birthday present. Your husband sent word it arrived on yesterday's train."

"My lands. I'd forgotten her birthday. Is it tomorrow?"

"It's today." Tom looked to his right. "Afternoon, Jeremiah."

He gave a nod in return. "Afternoon. Sarah's birthday, huh?"

"Yes."

"Well, give her my best wishes."

"I'll do it." Tom looked at Leslie, a wide grin brightening his face. "Did you see what I got her?"

"No. George put everything that came in the stockroom."

"It's a bicycle."

"A bicycle? Land o' Goshen! That'll set a few folks on their ears." She glanced at Jeremiah. "Can you imagine Sarah McNeal riding down Main Street on such a contraption?"

He gave another shrug. Truth was, he *could* imagine Sarah on a bicycle. He could imagine much more than that. He could imagine her in a hundred different ways, in a hundred different settings. Thinking about her was one of the reasons he slept so little at night.

"From the look of it," Tom said, bringing Jeremiah's attention back to him, "she won't be riding it any time soon. Not with all the snow we've got. But she'll enjoy it come spring."

"Will you still be here then?" Jeremiah asked.

"I leave for the East at the end of March. Maybe we'll have an early thaw and time to dry out so I can help her learn to ride it before I go."

Winter usually lingered in this high valley long after the calendar called it spring. Jeremiah remembered that well, and he supposed Tom remembered it too.

"And if I'm not here," Tom continued, "maybe you can help her."

"Me? I don't know anything about riding a bike."

"You'll figure it out. I trust you."

Tom trusted Jeremiah. But *could* he be trusted? *Should* he be trusted? Probably not. Not when it came to Sarah.

He looked toward Leslie. "Go ahead and wait on Tom. I'll

come back for my supplies later." He bent his hat brim in Tom's direction. "Like I said, give Sarah my best."

"I'll do it. You know, if you—"

"I need to get on with my rounds." He turned on his heel and left the mercantile.

Outside, he stopped on the boardwalk and drew in a deep breath, glad he'd gotten away before Tom could invite him over for Sarah's birthday. The last thing the gossips needed was to see him coming and going from the McNeal home. Especially not while Warren was still in Boulder Creek.

He headed west along the boardwalk, making his way beyond the hotel and the barber shop and the livery. Some kids played in the snow in a field to the north of Main Street, but mostly the town was quiet. Too quiet. It allowed his thoughts to drift to places they shouldn't go. To thoughts of Sarah.

He quickened his pace as he headed back through town toward the jail, but as he passed Madeline's Ladies Shop, a stripe of yellow caught his attention. He stopped and looked through the window glass at the straw hat. A moment later, he found himself opening the door.

"My goodness," Madeline Gaunt said when she saw him. "Deputy West, what brings you to my shop?"

"Nothing. I...I was just taking my usual turn about town."

The woman cocked an eyebrow.

He started to turn, intending to leave, but instead said, "I like that hat in the window." He pointed.

"Oh, yes. The Avery. It's a pretty one, don't you think?" She went to the display and picked up the blue and yellow hat, then turned to show it to him. "Just look how wonderfully it's made. Fancy straw braid and fine silk ribbons. See how real these velvet flowers look. Of course, it's not suitable for winter, but I couldn't leave it in the back a moment longer. The colors make me think of spring. I'm tired of cold and snow, and I thought these lovely colors might brighten things for others, too."

The pale yellow ribbons reminded him of Sarah's hair. The blue flowers were the same color as her eyes.

"How much is it?"

Madeline checked the tiny price tag pinned to the back of the hat. "Two dollars and seventy-five cents."

"I'll take it." He reached into his pocket and pulled out the money.

The woman's eyes widened. "This will make a nice gift for a young lady." Her expression begged him to tell her who that young lady was.

He should have told her to forget it. He should have told her to keep the hat. He should have lit out of that lady's shop like a dog with firecrackers tied to its tail.

He should have, but he didn't.

Jeremiah paid for the hat and took it to his room above the jail. He sat on the side of his bed, staring at the straw hat with its ribbons and flowers and imagining it perched upon Sarah's head, all the while wondering why he'd bought a gift for a woman he wanted so desperately to forget.

With a slow shake of his head, he put the hat away and slid the box beneath the bed, deciding it was one birthday present Sarah would never receive.

SARAH CARRIED A TEA TRAY INTO HER GRANDFATHER'S STUDY WHERE she found him seated in a leather chair near the window reading a book.

"Am I disturbing you?" she asked when he looked up.

"Not at all. Not at all." He closed the book and set it on the small table beside him.

"I thought you might like some tea."

"Sounds good."

She set down the tray, and once both of them had a cup of steaming tea in hand, she settled onto a stool near his chair. "What were you reading?"

"*Captains Courageous.*"

"Rudyard Kipling?"

"Yes."

"Is it good?"

"It is."

She glanced toward the study door. "Where's Tom?"

"Not sure. Stepped out for a bit. Probably with Doc."

"Or maybe he's getting my surprise." Smiling, she met Grandpa's gaze.

"Surprise?"

She laughed. "Has there ever been a year when you forgot my birthday? You or Tom. But neither of you have wished me a happy birthday today." She touched his cheek with her free hand. "That can only mean you're trying to surprise me."

A chuckle rumbled in his chest. "You're too sharp for us. Tom will be disappointed."

"I'll pretend to be surprised." Again she glanced toward the door. "But there's no cake. We're not prepared for guests."

"Your guests are in on the surprise. They'll bring everything we need for a party."

Sarah took a sip of tea, then set the cup aside before leaning her head on her grandfather's thigh. "Spending my birthday with you and Tom is all the party I need."

"Nonsense. Young people should always have a party."

"I'm twenty-two. I'm not a child."

He stroked a hand across her hair. "From where I'm sitting, twenty-two is awfully young."

They remained like that for a long while, her cheek resting

on his thigh, his hand stroking her head. All through her girl-hood, they'd spent times like this. The familiarity soothed her, comforted her, made her happy.

Breaking the silence, Grandpa said, "You aren't sorry, are you." His words were phrased like a question, yet they weren't. Nor did she need him to explain what he meant.

"No, I'm not." She straightened. "Grandma wasn't often wrong, but she was wrong about Warren and me. We wouldn't have done well together. We would never have learned to love each other."

Grandpa nodded. "I loved your grandmother a good many years. It's what I want for you." He sighed. "I'd like to see you married and happy before I go."

"You're not going anywhere."

He gave her a tolerant smile. "Not anytime soon. I hope the good Lord will give me many more years on this earth."

"That's the only gift I'll ever need. Just to have you with me."

TWENTY-THREE

The first weeks of the new year passed slowly. Perhaps it seemed slow because Sarah wanted to learn to ride the new bicycle that waited in the shed behind the house. Or perhaps it seemed slow because each day was much the same as the one before.

Warren departed Boulder Creek without saying goodbye to Sarah or her grandfather. She didn't know for certain, but she suspected he hadn't said goodbye to Jeremiah either.

If the people of Boulder Creek continued to gossip about the reason for Sarah's broken engagement, she didn't hear about it. She supposed it helped that Jeremiah never came to the McNeal home and was never seen talking to her. The most she received from him was a nod before or after church.

She yearned for more. It didn't seem to matter that he didn't speak to her or come to Sunday dinners. Still, he filled her thoughts. He filled them as she cleaned house and made supper for Grandpa and Tom, and he invaded her dreams when she slept at night.

And so the weeks of January passed.

Grandpa frowned as Sarah set a jar of jam in the center of the table. "You're looking kind of peaked this morning. Are you feeling poorly?"

"I didn't sleep well last night is all."

"Well, eat a hearty breakfast." Her grandfather slid the platter of fried eggs toward her. "It'll put some color back in those cheeks of yours."

Sarah's stomach lurched, and she swallowed the bile that rose in her throat. "I need fresh air." She hurried from the dining room, grabbing her coat on her way out the back door.

Temperatures above freezing the day before had softened the snow, but the night air had frozen it again into a hazardous path of small hills and ruts. Sarah tripped and nearly fell as she rushed toward the outhouse. She barely made it inside before she emptied her stomach. When the spasms ceased, she sank to the floor, tears streaking her cheeks, her legs drawn up to her chest.

"Sarah?" Tom's voice was accompanied by a rap on the outhouse door. "You okay?"

She sniffed and wiped her watering eyes with cold fingertips. "Yes."

After a few moments, her brother eased the door open. Silently, he handed her his handkerchief.

"Thanks." She blew her nose. "I don't know what came over me."

"Maybe we'd better have Doc take a look at you."

"It's nothing. I'm feeling better already." She started to rise, but her legs had weakened and she fell against the wall.

Tom grabbed her arm and helped her stand upright. "You'd better go back to bed."

"Don't be silly. I'll be fine." She took a step toward him,

then covered her mouth with a hand and turned away from him, fighting for control.

"You aren't all right, and you are going back to bed."

She drew a deep breath, then another. Finally, she said, "Are you going to speak to all your patients like that, Dr. McNeal?"

"Only the ones who don't do as they're told."

She pressed her hand against her unsettled stomach. "Then I'll go to bed." She faced Tom once again and offered a tremulous smile. "Some of Grandma's cider and ash remedy, and I'll be myself in an hour or two."

His expression grim, her brother took her by the arm and slowly guided her back to the house.

JEREMIAH GLANCED UP FROM THE FOOD ON HIS PLATE JUST AS TOM McNeal entered Zoe's. The younger man's gaze swept the cozy restaurant, stopping when he found Doc Varney seated with his wife at a table not far from Jeremiah. Tom quickly made his way through the other tables, conversations ceasing around him as he passed.

"Doc, you need to come have a look at Sarah."

Jeremiah set down his fork.

Tom lowered his voice. "She's sick."

Jeremiah's pulse hiccuped.

"What's wrong?" the doctor asked.

"She can't keep anything down. Been sick off and on all morning."

Doc Varney stood, setting the cloth napkin on the table. "Any fever?"

"No, sir. Not yet anyway."

The doctor looked at his wife. "Sorry, Betsy. I'd best see to the girl." Then to Tom, he said, "I'll get my bag and head over to your house."

Jeremiah wanted to follow Tom and the doctor out the door. He wanted to see Sarah for himself. But, of course, he couldn't allow himself to give into his wants. For five long weeks, he'd stayed away from Sarah for her sake. He'd even put a stop to her delivering a basket lunch to the jail. Best not to show an interest in her now.

He picked up the fork and took a bite of chicken. Not that he tasted it. It could have been sawdust he put in his mouth for all he knew. It wasn't Zoe's or the chicken's fault. He'd lost his appetite the instant he heard Tom say Sarah wasn't well.

After one more bite, he gave up the pretense of eating. He took money from his pocket and set it on the table next to his plate, then left the restaurant. Pulling up his coat collar against the cold, he walked toward the jail. His footsteps slowed when he came to North Street, and he looked in the direction of the McNeal house. Not that there was anything to see, other than a man on horseback, headed south out of town. No sign of Tom or Doc.

Was Sarah seriously ill? When he'd seen her at church on Sunday, she'd seemed herself, strong again, her struggle in the blizzard only a memory. Any illness couldn't be related to the storm. What had Tom said? She couldn't keep food down?

If he could see her now, he—

"Deputy West!"

He turned.

Grady Rourke, owner of the Pony Saloon, motioned him forward. "We've got trouble!" He jerked his head toward the doors of the saloon.

Jeremiah moved toward the man with quick strides. If the trouble was bad enough for Grady to call for his help, it was serious.

His instincts proved correct. When he entered the saloon, he found men frozen in place, some at tables, some at the bar. All of them looked in the same direction. He followed their gazes to a corner near the piano where a young man held a knife to the throat of one of the saloon girls. Her eyes were wide, her terror obvious even from a distance.

"Grady," Jeremiah said, "who is he?"

"I don't know. Never seen him before today. Must've come in on the train."

"What's he got against the girl?"

"Nothing that I know of. He was playing poker with a couple regulars. There was a disagreement. Not sure about what. Hawkins pulled a knife, and the kid took it from him. He got a bad slice on the hand, judging by the blood on the floor."

Jeremiah gave a soft grunt to indicate he was listening.

"Next thing we knew, he grabbed Fanny and said she was coming with him. But he couldn't get by the others and they ended up in that corner."

Jeremiah nodded, then took a step forward. "Mister, it's time for you to let the lady go."

"Don't come near me."

"Come on. You've got no call to hurt her."

"I do. She was helping him cheat me." He motioned with the knife toward Hawkins. "She was giving him signals, letting him know what kind of hand I had."

Jeremiah took another step forward. "If that's true, the law will handle it. But you'll have to let her go first."

Fanny released a tiny squeal as the man tightened his arm around her waist and pressed the knife closer to her throat.

"I'm Deputy West," Jeremiah said quickly. "What's your name?"

"Don't matter."

"It does to me."

The fellow with the knife wasn't much more than twenty, if that. A kid, like Grady had called him. There was a glint of desperation in his eyes, but he didn't seem to be intoxicated. That was good. Liquor never made a dangerous situation better. Trouble was, the kid was boxed into a corner. He was too far from an exit, and there were too many men in the saloon itching to take him down should he relinquish the girl. If any of them tried to take him by force, there was no telling what would happen. To the girl. To the kid.

He drew a slow breath and dared another step closer. "I'll call you Joe. Is that all right?"

The young man gave a slight jerk of his head. "The name's Rafe."

Jeremiah looked at the girl. "Fanny, are you okay?"

Her eyes widened even more, and another squeak slipped from her lips.

"Rafe, can you feel her shaking? She's afraid." Another step took him beyond the last table. If he reached out, he could touch the piano. "Even if she did what you think she did, you've got no call to frighten her like this. You don't want to hurt her." He lowered his voice. "You really don't want to hurt her. Even if you're right about what she did, hurting her is the wrong choice."

Something flickered in the young man's eyes. A wish to be out of his predicament? Jeremiah hoped so and held out his hand, palm up. "Let Fanny go and give me the knife." He eased forward. "Make the right choice."

A few tense moments passed, and then Fanny stumbled free of her captor's arms. A cry escaped her as Jeremiah took her arm and drew her around behind him until she was out of danger. Then he released his grip and she fled.

A corresponding grumble of male voices told Jeremiah that

the danger wasn't over yet. Not for the kid who remained in the corner, knife in hand.

"Look at me." As soon as he had Rafe's attention, he said, "I'm going to take you over to the sheriff's office now so we can have a talk. Just you and me."

He didn't expect the young man to do as he was told. He'd feared a struggle might be involved. But then he saw the fight go out of the kid's eyes. He stepped close and took the knife from Rafe's hand.

A grumble of voices caused him to look behind him. A few men had moved toward the piano.

"Stay where you are." He glared at them. "I've got this."

Then without delay, he escorted Rafe out of the saloon. But he didn't draw a steady breath until he and the kid were inside the sheriff's office, the door closed tightly behind them.

TWENTY-FOUR

J eremiah knocked on the McNeal door. It wasn't long before Tom opened it. "Is Doc still here?"

"Yes. He's with Sarah."

Everything in Jeremiah wanted to ask how she was. Instead, he said, "I've got a prisoner with a bad cut on his hand. It needs stitches."

"Come on in." Tom stepped back from the opening.

It had been more than a month since Jeremiah last entered this house. Coming inside felt like coming home. A ridiculous notion. He hadn't been cut off from the McNeals. Not completely. He'd talked to Hank whenever the sheriff came into the office. He'd talked to Tom when he'd run into him around town. He'd exchanged nods with Sarah after church. It was enough.

"I don't think Doc will be much longer." Tom led the way into the parlor.

"I should go back to the jail. I can wait for him there. I don't want to intrude." Before he could turn and leave, the click of boot heels on the stairs drew his gaze.

Doc and Hank descended from the second floor, their expressions grim. Alarm sounded in Jeremiah's heart.

The sheriff's brows lifted. "Jeremiah."

"Sorry to disturb, sir. I've got an injured prisoner. Needs the doctor's attention when he can come." His gaze lifted toward the top of the stairs, and the question he was dying to ask slipped out. "How's Sarah?"

"She's a sick girl," Doc Varney answered, "but she'll be all right."

"What...what is it?"

"I reckon she ate something gone bad."

With a shake of his head, Hank said, "Can't think what she ate that we didn't." His gaze went to Tom, who nodded in agreement. "Why aren't we sick, too?"

"No telling on that. We'll keep an eye on her." Doc stepped toward Jeremiah. "But for now, let's go have a look at your prisoner."

Jeremiah didn't want to leave. Not until he knew for certain that Sarah was all right. But he had no choice. She wasn't his responsibility. After a quick nod at Hank and Tom, he followed the doctor out the door. They made their way in silence until they were passing the schoolyard.

"Doc, is Miss McNeal really going to be all right?"

"Yes. I've seen this sort of thing before, and it usually runs its course in a day or two. Not pleasant but not serious either."

He thought of Marta. The doctor in Iowa hadn't thought her illness anything serious either, but she and their baby had died all the same. After that, Jeremiah had lost faith in most physicians, no matter how likable the man might be. Doc Varney was likable, but was he right about Sarah?

The two men crossed Main Street and soon entered the sheriff's office. Jeremiah led the way to the back room where he opened the cell door for the doctor. Rafe sat on the cot, his wrapped hand held upward.

"Let me have a look at that, shall we?" Doc pulled a stool close to the cot.

"Do you need anything from me?" Jeremiah asked.

"No, son. I've got what I need."

"Holler when you're ready to leave."

He twisted the key in the lock, then returned to the front office. The desk held some flyers he should look through, and it wouldn't hurt to clean his gun and the rifles stored behind the desk. But he moved to the window instead. The snow that blanketed Boulder Creek was no longer a pristine white. Time, foot and horse traffic, and temperatures that rose above freezing during the day and fell below freezing at night had seen to that.

I should go back to the farm. The roads are passable. I don't have to stay in town.

His gaze went in the direction of the McNeal house. He couldn't see it from this vantage point, but that didn't matter. He knew it was there.

His mind went to the night of the blizzard and to the memory of Sarah, lying close to the stove, shivering from the cold. He remembered holding her and doing his best to warm her, praying for her survival. Now she was sick again, and he couldn't be with her. He shouldn't want to be with her. He had no right to be with her.

Did he want to have that right?

Warren was out of the picture, gone from Boulder Creek for good. The gossip had died down about the reason for the broken engagement. But even if Jeremiah cared for Sarah, it couldn't lead anywhere. He'd made up his mind a long time ago about that. Long before he'd ever laid eyes on Sarah McNeal.

Maybe he should leave Boulder Creek. Forget the farm. Just hit the road again.

"Jeremiah." Doc's voice jerked him to the present. "I'm finished here."

"Be right there." He grabbed the key off the hook.

If he didn't keep his mind on his job, he might as well leave town. He would be no good for anyone.

SARAH OPENED HER EYES TO SEE HER GRANDFATHER SITTING ON THE chair beside the bed.

"Tom said you're feeling better." He took hold of her hand.

"A little."

"Feel ready to try some chicken broth? Mrs. Jacobs brought over a pot when she heard you'd taken ill."

Sarah moved her head slowly on the pillow. "Not yet, Grandpa."

"Well, at least take a sip of water." He held out a cup.

With a faint smile, she obliged him.

"Knock, knock."

She looked toward the door.

Rosalie Randolph stepped into the bedroom. "Tom told me it would be all right to come up. Do you mind a visitor?"

Two hours ago, Sarah would have sent Rosalie away. No one wanted company while retching into a pot. But her stomach had calmed, and the room was no longer spinning. "Please come in."

Grandpa stood and motioned for Rosalie to take the chair. "I'll leave you ladies alone."

"I don't want to chase you away, Mr. McNeal."

"You aren't." With a smile, he left the room.

Settled on the chair, Rosalie looked at Sarah again. "I'm

thankful you're feeling better. I was worried when I heard how ill you were. You haven't had enough time to recover from your ordeal in the storm."

Sarah wanted to argue, but she hadn't the strength. And that would only seem to confirm Rosalie's words. Instead, she asked, "How did you hear I was sick?"

"Ma told me. I don't know who told her. Somebody who was at Zoe's when Tom went looking for Doc, I suppose."

"Everyone at Zoe's heard I was sick?" Sarah groaned as she closed her eyes. "How busy was the restaurant? Were you there?" She hated the thought of giving the gossips something new to talk about, even if it was a minor illness.

Rosalie covered Sarah's hand with hers on the bed. "Don't mind what others have to say. Besides, most folk will only share their concern for you."

"I hope you're right." She looked at her friend. "But you can't understand. You weren't the center of gossip for most of the winter."

"Maybe not this winter, but I've been gossiped about in the past."

"You?" Sarah dared to scoot herself up in the bed, thankful that the effort didn't start the room spinning again.

"Me."

"When was that?"

"Soon after Michael came to Boulder Creek."

Sarah searched her memory, but she couldn't recall any gossip about Rosalie. Of course, she'd been a girl of twelve or thirteen when Michael Randolph came to town to build his hotel. Her head had been in the clouds or her nose in a book. She'd had no time for the gossip of old wives and silly girls.

"We were strangers caught in a...a compromising situation."

"You were strangers?"

"It wasn't what it looked like, but my pa said it was. He forced us to marry."

Sarah felt her eyes widen even more.

"Michael didn't have to do what Pa wanted. He could have refused. We hadn't done anything wrong. Like I said, we were strangers. He was a boarder in Ma's boarding house." A gentle smile bowed her lips. "But I'm ever so grateful that he didn't refuse to marry me because Michael and the children are the greatest blessings in my life. I shudder to think what would have happened to me without him as my husband."

"I didn't know. I wouldn't have guessed. You two are so in love. Everyone respects you. Why, Michael's even been elected mayor."

"The gossip was bad at first. But eventually the attention moved on from us. There was something new of interest. Time helps."

"You're telling me the gossips will find someone new to talk about if I just wait."

Rosalie squeezed Sarah's fingers, then released her hand. "Yes, that's what I'm telling you."

Energy spent, Sarah slid down on the bed and her eyes drifted closed.

"I'll leave you to rest." Rosalie patted Sarah's shoulder. "I'll come to see you tomorrow."

"Thank you for coming."

She wasn't awake to hear the closing of the door.

TWENTY-FIVE

Melting snow trickled from the eaves of the farmhouse. One large drop landed on Jeremiah's uncovered head and slid down the back of his neck. Shivering, he grabbed the firewood he'd come for. As he turned around, he heard the approach of a horse and waited to see if the rider would pass by on the way north or turn in to the farm lane. When the latter proved true, he set the firewood on a bench near the door and waited to see his visitor.

Tom McNeal rode into view seconds later, his expression grave.

Alarm shouted Sarah's name in Jeremiah's chest. "Is there trouble in town?"

Tom reined in. "No. Leastwise, not like you mean."

"Is it Sarah? Has her sickness worsened?"

Something flickered in Tom's eyes. Distrust? Anger? What? "Let's go inside."

"Of course." He drew Tom's horse to the hitching post and looped the reins around the rail. Then with another glance in

Tom's direction, he led the way inside, the firewood ignored. "Would you like some coffee to warm you?"

"No. Thanks."

Drawing a breath, he faced his visitor. "What is it? What's happened?"

Tom removed his hat and combed his fingers through his hair. "The talk's started up again."

"Talk?" he asked—but he knew what Tom meant.

"About you and Sarah."

"There's nothing—"

"Now there's talk she's...that she's having your...baby."

Jeremiah took a step back, feeling like Tom had punched him. "But there's no truth in it. She couldn't... We didn't—"

"I know." Tom sat on a chair. "I know my sister better than that. But remember how we found her in this house after the blizzard. I expect I wasn't the only man to notice her clothes drying by the fire. And then when she got sick, someone must have counted the weeks since the storm and decided what it meant."

Anger twisted in Jeremiah's gut. "Who started the rumor?"

"I don't know. Does it matter?"

"Has Sarah heard what's being said?"

Tom shook his head. "Not yet. But she hasn't left the house since she took sick. She's bound to hear eventually. Mrs. Randolph thinks we should tell her now."

Jeremiah swore softly as he walked to the window and stared out at the land beyond. This was his fault. He should have protected Sarah better. He'd distanced himself from her after Warren's harsh words at the social, but that hadn't been enough. What would have been enough?

"Grandpa thought you should know what's being said since it concerns you too."

He turned toward Tom. "He doesn't believe the gossip, does he?"

"No." The hint of a grim smile tugged at the corners of his mouth. "If Grandpa believed the rumor, he'd be here instead of me. And he would have a different way of settling things besides talking."

"How do we fix it?"

"Not sure. Time will eventually dispel the part that she's pregnant. Not sure anything will help the notion that something inappropriate happened. Not after what Warren said."

"How could anybody believe it about Sarah? She hasn't got a wicked bone in her body. Who would want to hurt her that way?"

"I don't know." Tom stood. "Maybe somebody who's jealous of her."

Jeremiah bit back a curse. More than that, he wanted to hit something. Or someone.

Tom moved toward the door. "Will we see you at church in the morning?"

"I'll be there."

Once he was alone, Jeremiah sat, his thoughts roiling. His anger felt hotter than the fire in the stove nearby. Why would anybody be so cruel to Sarah? She'd done nothing wrong.

He pictured women in the mercantile, whispering behind their hands. Whispering about Sarah. For what? For surviving? After nearly freezing to death in a blizzard, she'd been rescued. That was her crime.

If anyone was to blame for anything it was him, not her. He was the one who'd brought her into his house. He was the one who'd disrobed her and done all he could to keep her warm and dry. Innocent, it might have been, but if aspersions needed to be cast, he was the guilty party. Not her.

The need to rescue Sarah from a different kind of storm welled in Jeremiah's chest. But how? How could he help her when he was the cause of her trouble in the first place?

———

THE CLOCK ON THE PARLOR MANTEL TICKED LOUDLY. SARAH LOOKED from her grandfather to her brother to Rosalie, then back to her grandfather again. A buzzing filled her ears. Her body felt numb.

"But there's not a shred of truth to it," she whispered.

Grandpa harrumphed.

"We know that," Tom said for them both.

Rosalie got up and came to sit on the sofa beside Sarah. "You'll weather this."

"I knew some people thought harshly of me for calling off the wedding, but I never thought anyone would be—" Her breath caught in her throat, and she couldn't continue.

A knock sounded at the front door.

Sarah winced and closed her eyes. It was bad enough looking at her family and her close friend. She didn't want to see anyone else. Not now. Not when she knew what was being whispered about her.

Tom said, "I'll send them away."

Thank you, she thought, grateful for his understanding.

The mantel clock chimed the hour. Only three o'clock? It felt as if they'd been in this room for hours and hours.

"Sarah?"

She opened her eyes. Someone stood behind Tom in the entrance to the parlor. Wasn't her brother supposed to send the visitor away? Why hadn't he done as he said? Then Tom stepped into the room, revealing Jeremiah. Her heart skipped a beat.

"Sarah," he said, "I hoped we could talk."

Tears welled in her eyes as she shook her head.

"Please."

Strange, wasn't it? The way his tender plea caused her heart to nearly break in two. She'd missed him over these past weeks. She'd missed taking lunch to him at the jail. She'd missed seeing him at the McNeal table after church on Sundays. She'd missed the sound of his voice and the gentle rumble of his laughter. She'd missed the way he'd look at her across a room. She barely knew him and yet it seemed she knew him better than anyone in the world.

"Yes. We can talk." She stood.

Jeremiah looked at her grandfather. "May we use your study, sir?"

"If she's of a mind to," Grandpa answered, his voice deep with emotion.

Sarah remembered asking Warren into her grandfather's study so she could break their engagement. Was Jeremiah about to deliver bad news of his own? Would he leave Boulder Creek now? And why wouldn't he go? He wasn't deserving of the gossip. She might be, because of Warren, but he wasn't. He could sell his land. There was nothing to tie him to this town now. With his brother living in Boise, Jeremiah had no family left in Boulder Creek. Why stay?

Blinking back another wave of tears, she led the way to the study where she sat on the nearest chair, her eyes downcast, waiting for whatever bad news he might deliver.

"Tom came to the farm to see me earlier today."

She nodded.

"I'm sorry there's been talk. I'm sorry you've been hurt by the cruelty of others."

"It isn't your fault." She met his gaze. "You did nothing but try to help me."

The look in his eyes was tender. In response, a lump formed in her throat.

"Sarah, I would like to ask your grandfather for your hand in marriage."

She sucked in a gasp of surprise.

"I know there is no love between us, and I'd not expect it. But we seem to get on well enough. Friendship can grow from that. Friendship between a husband and wife is a good thing. And if we marry, perhaps it will quiet tongues."

"Or perhaps it will make people think they were right about us, that something...inappropriate...happened. It might convince people even more that a baby's on the way." Her cheeks grew hot, but she forced herself to hold his gaze.

"That's possible. But as your husband, I can put a stop to the gossip."

His words almost made her smile. *Almost.* Did he truly think he could control the thoughts and tongues of others?

Jeremiah pulled a second chair close to her and sat on it. Forearms on his thighs, he leaned toward her, his gaze holding hers. "Sarah, let me do this for you. Marry me. It would give you a home away from town, away from the gossips. I'll never be rich, but I'll never let you do without either. I won't let you be at risk. I won't ask for what you can't give, and I won't...I won't fail you the way I failed Marta."

Marta. Did he still love her? The question gave her pause.

Jeremiah reached to take one of her hands. "Say yes."

He wanted to rescue her again. He didn't love her, but he wanted to protect her. He was good and he was kind.

And I love him.

Should she tell him how she felt? He thought there was no love between them. Should she let him know he was wrong? That he'd won her heart without trying.

"Sarah?"

"Yes."

He studied her with that intense gaze of his.

"Yes, Jeremiah, I will marry you."

TWENTY-SIX

On Sunday, soon after the regular service ended and the congregation departed, Jeremiah stood beside Sarah at the front of the sanctuary and pledged that he would be her wedded husband, that he would have and hold her, from that day forward, for better, for worse, for richer, for poorer, in sickness and in health. He promised to love and to cherish her until death parted them.

Did she wince a little when he promised to love her? Or was he the one who winced when he spoke the words about death?

"What God has joined together, let no man put asunder." Reverend Jacobs closed his prayer book. "Jeremiah, you may kiss your bride."

He looked down at Sarah. They'd never kissed before. Did she want him to kiss her now?

She glanced in the reverend's direction, then back at him.

Yes, he should kiss her. If for no other reason than the few witnesses in the sanctuary. Refusing to do so might embarrass her, and he didn't want that.

He bent forward and brushed her mouth with his lips. When he pulled back, he saw the glitter of tears in her eyes. They were accompanied by a smile. Despite himself, he felt warmed by the response. He wanted Sarah to be happy. They wouldn't have a conventional marriage, but he wouldn't fail her the way he'd failed Marta. He'd sworn to himself that he wouldn't. He'd promised before God.

The reverend cleared his throat. "Congratulations, Jeremiah, Sarah. I wish you both every happiness."

"Thank you," Sarah whispered, a faint blush in her cheeks.

In unison, they turned to face the four witnesses to their union.

Hank stepped forward and kissed Sarah's cheek before shaking Jeremiah's hand. "Be good to her."

"I will, sir."

Tom followed his grandfather's actions, but there was a look of worry in his eyes. As if he wasn't sure his sister had done the right thing.

Jeremiah wondered the same.

Rosalie and Michael Randolph were the last to congratulate the bride and groom. And when that was done, there was nothing left for Jeremiah to do except gather his bride and her belongings and go to the farm.

As the small party left the church and made their way to the McNeal home, Jeremiah looked only at his bride, his right hand cupping her left elbow, while she stared at the ground before her. He knew people watched from behind curtains. He knew the whispers hadn't stopped the moment others learned there was to be a wedding. But they would stop soon enough. Jeremiah wouldn't let anyone say unkind things about his wife. He would shelter her. He would die to protect her.

Hank opened the front door of the house, then stepped aside to allow them entrance.

"I've packed some things," Sarah said, looking up at Jeremiah. "I'll get them." She slipped from his grasp and hurried toward the stairs.

Anxiety knotted his gut as he watched her go. Would he fail her? Would he make her unhappy? Had he done the right thing?

"You're a fool, Jeremiah. You'll never amount to anything." He closed his eyes, as if that would block out his father's voice in his head.

A hand rested on his shoulder. "Son, keep the faith."

He looked at Hank and gave a brief nod.

"She's a strong girl, my Sarah. She knows her mind."

"Yes, sir."

"If you let her, she'll make you happy."

Jeremiah nodded again. Although his own happiness wasn't the issue. Not for him.

SARAH LOOKED AROUND HER BEDROOM, MEMORIES FLOODING OVER her. The times she'd sat in the window seat and shared with her grandmother about her dreams of traveling the world. The nights she'd lain in bed and read books about exotic places and exciting people until the wee hours of the morning. Memories of a girlhood filled with warmth and love. A bittersweet smile tugged at the corners of her mouth as she bid the room—and her girlhood—a silent farewell.

I'm married. I'm married to Jeremiah.

Tears filled her eyes, but she blinked them back. This was not a day for crying. This was a day for joy. She'd married the man she loved, although he didn't know it, although he didn't seem to want it. But that could change. Look at Rosalie and

Michael. Their love was obvious for all to see. Yet they'd been little but strangers at the start of their marriage.

I'll teach him to love me. She crossed her arms over her chest, closed her eyes, and drew in a deep breath. *I'll earn his love, and until then, I'll love enough for the both of us.*

Opening her eyes, she lifted her satchel off the floor. The bag wasn't heavy. Only a few things were inside: a second dress, a change of underclothes, another pair of stockings, a bar of scented soap from the Montgomery Ward catalogue, her toothbrush and a tin of saleratus for cleaning her teeth, her grandmother's silver handled hairbrush and mirror, and a nightgown.

A nightgown.

A wedding night.

Strange sensations swirled in her belly. Not fear. Not dread. Something she couldn't name. Anticipation, perhaps?

Drawing a shaky breath, she gripped the satchel tighter and left her childhood bedroom.

Tom waited for her at the bottom of the stairs, but her grandfather and Jeremiah were nowhere in sight. She stopped in front of her brother and waited as he leaned in and kissed her cheek. "I hope you'll be happy, Sarah."

"I will."

"The sleigh's waiting for you."

"I know. I saw it from the landing."

"Grandpa and I put together some supplies. Flour, sugar, meat, some canned vegetables, a couple of frying pans. We thought Jeremiah might not have had a chance to stock up since he hasn't stayed out there much."

"Thank you." She blinked back unexpected tears. "Take care of Grandpa for me."

"You know I will."

"Yes."

Her grandfather and Jeremiah appeared in the parlor arch-way. Sarah's pulse quickened. Her groom looked so handsome in his black suit, his face clean-shaven, his hair slicked back.

Jeremiah stepped forward. "We should be on our way."

She nodded.

"Are you ready?"

Was she ready? Ready to begin a new life. Ready to be a deputy's wife, a farmer's wife. Ready to love this dark-haired man with his intense gaze.

"Yes," she answered. "I'm ready."

THE FORTY-FIVE MINUTE JOURNEY TO THE WEST FARM WAS A SILENT one. Jeremiah felt Sarah glance his way occasionally, but he kept his gaze fastened to the road. He wasn't ready to begin a conversation. Nerves tied his belly in knots. He felt like a fumbling boy of fifteen all of a sudden.

As the ground swished by beneath the runners on the sleigh, Jeremiah let his thoughts slip back across the weeks since he'd returned to Boulder Creek. Memories of Sarah flooded his mind. He pictured her at church, in her home, in the sheriff's office, along the boardwalk, in the snow, and on the floor of his house, shivering beside the fire. He cared for her, cared more than he wanted to care, more than he should care. It would be far wiser to keep his heart closed to her. But Sarah had a way of making him forget the plans he'd made.

He would need to be careful if he was to keep his promises.

At last, the farmhouse came into view. A few minutes later, he drew the horse to a halt near the front door. "Here we are." He turned his head to look at her.

She stared at the house, as if seeing it for the first time.

Was it the first time? He wondered. Maybe she'd never

come calling at the West house. Warren had lived in town in recent years so there would have been no reason for Sarah to ride out this way. When she'd stumbled into the barn on the night of the blizzard, she couldn't have seen the house at all. When the search team had taken her back to Boulder Creek, she'd been barely aware of her surroundings. Did she look at the farmhouse now and compare it to the one she'd left in town? If so, her new home would be found wanting. How long would it be before she regretted her decision to marry him?

He hopped down from the sleigh, then helped his bride to the ground after him. He led her the few steps to the door and opened it for her, motioning for her to enter before him. The interior was dim, the air cool.

"I'll make a fire in the stove." He closed the door behind him. "It won't take long to warm the room."

"You didn't stay at the farm last night?"

"No. I slept above the jail." He opened the grate on the stove and added kindling and firewood. "Didn't make much sense for me to ride back to the farm, then turn around again in the morning. Didn't think there was anything I needed to do here." After retrieving a box of matches from a shelf, he squatted again in front of the stove and struck a match. "I should have realized how cold it would be when you got here. I'm sorry."

"I don't mind, Jeremiah. My coat is warm. And the fire will be blazing soon."

As if in response to her words, the kindling caught and tiny flames began to lick the fuel inside the stove.

"I'll get my things from the sleigh," she said.

He stood and turned. "No. You stay put. I'll bring everything inside and then take care of the horse."

A disappointed look crossed her face, but a moment later she lifted her chin and gave him a brief smile.

He was making a mess of this. Why hadn't he thought it through? He'd offered her marriage to protect her from the gossips, not to make her even more miserable.

"It won't take me long." With that, he hurried outside.

Two trips was all it took to bring in her satchel, one medium sized trunk, and a box of supplies. The satchel and trunk he set on the floor near the door. The box he carried to the kitchen table.

Sarah removed her coat before joining him in the kitchen. "Do you care where I put things?" She began lifting items from the box and setting them on the table next to it.

The question stopped him for a moment. He hadn't thought about organizing the kitchen. He hadn't considered where to put the flour or where to put pots and pans. He'd kept everything in the same place his father had. But this would be her kitchen now. She would want it orderly and to her liking. The way most wives did.

Most wives.

"Jeremiah?"

"Put it wherever you like."

With a nod in her direction, he headed outside to tend to the horse. By the time the animal was out of the harness, rubbed down, watered and fed, clouds had rolled in, darkening the sky. There was no threat of a storm in them. They served only to cast a gray pall over the earth.

"You're a fool, Jeremiah. You'll never amount to anything."

He looked toward the house and prayed his father wasn't right.

TWENTY-SEVEN

When Jeremiah opened the door, he was met with delicious odors wafting from the kitchen. While he'd been outside, Sarah had made a fire in the cook stove, and something sizzled in the skillet atop the stove. None of the supplies lingered on the table. Apparently everything had found its place.

He closed the door with the heel of his boot, and the sound drew Sarah's gaze. Her smile was hesitant.

She'd tied a faded apron from the hook on the wall over her blue dress. Wisps of pale hair had pulled free from the cluster of curls at the back of her head, falling about her shoulders in long coils. His pulse quickened at the sight of her. No one as pretty as Sarah had stood in this kitchen before. Not ever. The desire to hold her in his arms and kiss her swept over him.

He was allowed to kiss her now. He was her husband. But would she welcome it if he tried? Maybe she would. But even so, he couldn't let it happen. The only sure way he could protect her—and himself—was to keep his distance.

"Something smells good," he said, the words sounding gruff in his ears.

"It's beefsteak and onions. It was with the supplies Grandpa sent. Nothing fancy but tasty." She turned to the stove. "It should be ready soon, if you want to wash up."

He moved to the sink.

"I put out a new bar of soap," she added. "Next to the pump."

A smile curved his mouth as he removed the tissue paper wrapping from the bay rum and glycerine soap. She must have brought this for him. Her own soap, he was certain, smelled of lavender. He'd caught the fragrance of it more than once when he'd been near her.

As he grasped the pump handle, he said a silent word of thanks that he could provide Sarah this small luxury. Not every house in the valley had an indoor pump. A few had no pump at all, instead depending upon the creek and rain for their water supply.

By the time Jeremiah turned from the sink, Sarah had placed plates, cups, and utensils on the table.

"Can I help?" he asked.

"No. Just sit yourself down. Dinner's ready."

He recalled the Sunday dinners he'd eaten with the McNeals and their friends. He recalled the linen tablecloth and the fine porcelain plates and cups and serving bowls. Sarah was used to nicer things. He should have thought of that before asking her to marry him and live on this farm.

"You're a fool, Jeremiah. You'll never amount to anything."

He clenched his jaw. Why did his father's angry words have to stick in his mind today? He thought he'd found a measure of peace since returning to Boulder Creek. He thought he'd resolved those hurt places in his heart. But today seemed to have stirred up old wounds. Maybe because he feared his dad was right about him. That he wouldn't amount to anything. He'd failed to keep Marta safe. Would he fail Sarah as well?

She set the platter of steak and onions on the table, breaking into his dark thoughts. He looked up as she sat opposite him and again was struck by her beauty and a feeling he couldn't quite define. Something more than desire.

Color rose in her cheeks as he continued to stare, reminding him of her innocence. What did she know of the intimacies of a marriage? He'd told her he didn't expect love. Had she understood what he'd meant?

"Would you say a blessing?" Sarah asked softly.

"Sure." He ducked his face and folded his hands.

Unlike some, Jeremiah hadn't learned to pray at his father's knee. There'd been no blessings said at the West dinner table. As a boy and young man, he'd believed in God in a general sense, but it was only after he married Marta that his heart had been touched by the truth of the gospel. In the book of First Peter it said a wife, by virtue of her obedience and without a word, could win an unbelieving husband to the truth, and that's what had happened to Jeremiah. Still, praying aloud wasn't easy for him. But Sarah had asked, so he would do it.

"Lord, thanks for this day and for the food You put before us. Bless Sarah's hands for preparing it. Amen."

"Amen."

After a few moments of silence, Sarah slid the platter closer to Jeremiah. Longing surged in him again, and it had nothing to do with the steak and onions he piled on his plate. He picked up his knife and fork, needing a distraction, but he waited to cut his first bite of meat until Sarah had her portion of the meal on her own plate.

"When I was a little girl," she said, "I used to pretend that Grandpa and Grandma were a duke and duchess and all the folks in Boulder Creek were the villagers. When there was a barn dance, I made believe all the people there were lords and ladies of the realm and the barn was a wondrous ballroom."

Although he wondered at the odd direction her thoughts had taken, he nodded to show he listened.

"I dreamed I would travel to see the places I'd read about in books and magazines. I especially wanted to see the Philadelphia Dancing Assembly." Eyes closed, she swayed from side to side, as if in time to music he couldn't hear.

"You had quite the imagination."

"I did." She opened her eyes and lifted her gaze to meet his. "I still do. But I'm learning to love the garden where God has planted me."

———

MORE THAN ANYTHING, SARAH HOPED JEREMIAH WOULD UNDERSTAND what she was trying to say to him. That God had planted her in his life and in this marriage. That he held her heart. That she didn't want to be anywhere else. Could he see that?

I love you, Jeremiah.

She wished she could say those words aloud, but her heart told her he wasn't ready to hear them. Not yet. But one day. She would be patient. She would have to be.

Clearing her throat, she asked, "What did you pretend when you were a boy?"

His expression cooled. "I didn't pretend. My dad had no patience for nonsense."

Nonsense? He thought what she'd shared with him was nonsense? She tried not to be hurt by his words, but she was.

She turned her attention to the food on her plate, and the two of them ate their simple wedding supper in silence. When finished, she rose to clear the table. Without her asking for his help, Jeremiah brought the kettle of hot water to the sink and emptied it into the wash basin. Sarah added cold water from the pump, then set to washing the dishes and frying pan.

"I'll put your things in the bedroom," Jeremiah said from behind her.

Tiny flutters erupted in her stomach. It was still mid-afternoon, but his words reminded her of the wedding night that awaited them. There was more to such a night than she understood, and the unknown left her nervous. Thankfully she had six hours or more to calm those nerves.

While she finished washing and drying the dishes, she listened to the sounds of Jeremiah moving about the house. The *creak* of the bedroom door. The *thump* of her trunk upon the floor. The crackle of fire as wood was added to the stove. Instead of decreasing, the nervous tension seemed to worsen by the minute.

"I've got a few chores to see to in the barn."

She turned to face him. "Do you need my help?"

"No." He motioned with his head. "You should settle in." He reached for his coat and headed outside.

Releasing a breath, Sarah looked around the kitchen. All was in order. Clean dishes had been put away. The table and counter had been wiped. She'd looked through the foodstuffs and made a mental note of what they should buy at the mercantile. They would need to have their own chickens too. It wasn't as if Sarah could go to buy things at the store at the last moment. She may have lived her life in town, but she wasn't completely ignorant of what would be required of a farmer's wife. And she wasn't afraid of hard work. What she didn't know, Jeremiah could teach her.

She walked to the bedroom door nearest the heating stove. It opened without a sound.

Sarah had a vague memory of coming into this bedroom on the morning after the blizzard, her brother holding her upright. She'd been wrapped in a blanket, and beneath the blanket, she'd worn a nightshirt. One that carried the masculine scent of Jeremiah, although she hadn't realized it at the time. Tom had helped her sit on the edge of the bed, then had turned his back while she changed into her own clothes. The effort had left her faint, and a short while later, Tom had lifted her into his arms and carried her out to the sleigh.

There was little she remembered about this room, and now she knew why. There was little to see. A bed with a couple of plain blankets covering the mattress. A lamp on a rough-hewn table at the side of the bed. The hat Jeremiah wore to church on Sundays hanging on a peg in the wall. A nightshirt hanging on a second peg. No curtain covered the window that was placed high on one wall, letting in a pale gray light.

Then she realized that her trunk and satchel weren't in the room. Where had he put them? They were no longer near the front door. Pulse quickening, she walked to the second bedroom. A familiar—and dreaded—*creak* met her ears as she opened the door. And there, on the floor at the foot of the bed, were her trunk and satchel.

"I won't ask for what you can't give." As Jeremiah's words whispered in her memory, she realized he didn't intend for them to share a room—or a bed. Something cold coiled in her heart as she dropped onto the edge of the bed and let her tears fall.

TWENTY-EIGHT

E arly the next morning, Jeremiah sat on a stool in the barn, rubbing soap into the leather harness. He worked it deep with his fingers, then buffed it with a soft cloth. But his mind wasn't on the leather or the business of cleaning it. His thoughts were on Sarah.

When he'd returned from the barn last night, Sarah had been in her room, the door closed. How he'd wanted to go to that door, to rap on it softly, to go into her as a groom was supposed to go into his bride. But he'd resisted the temptation. For her sake, he had to remain strong. He wouldn't allow the scandalmongers to think they'd been right about the night of the blizzard. A pregnancy would only fuel the cruel gossip. Nor would he risk Sarah's life by getting her with child. He wouldn't lose her the way he'd lost Marta.

Jeremiah hadn't known real love until he'd married Marta. For a few short years, his world had been a warm place to be. He'd loved her—and then he'd lost her. Her and the baby they'd made.

He stopped rubbing the leather and closed his eyes, head bowed.

From the moment Marta had told him she was expecting, fear had gnarled his belly. What did he have to give a child? He didn't know how to be a good dad. What if he was cold and remote like his own father? What if he was cruel? What if he failed his son or daughter, the way his dad had said he would? Was that why God took Marta and their child? Because he would have failed them.

Sarah's face drifted into his thoughts. Sweet, sweet Sarah with her hopes and dreams of a world beyond this valley. Sarah, who believed that all would be well. She'd offered him love. He'd seen it in her blue eyes. But he couldn't accept it, and he couldn't offer it to her in return.

Because losing Sarah was something he could not bear.

———

SARAH AWAKENED TO A SPLASH OF SUNSHINE SPILLING THROUGH THE bedroom window. How had she let herself sleep so late? What would Jeremiah think of her, sleeping away the morning.

After washing and dressing, she hurried from the bedroom, ready to apologize to her new husband. But she discovered Jeremiah wasn't in the house. His coat was gone from the peg near the door. He must be busy with his morning chores. She should do the same.

In the kitchen, she found a kettle of water already heating on the stove as well as a pot of freshly-brewed coffee. She took a cup from the shelf and filled it with the dark liquid. Next, she opened a jar of peach preserves and spread some on a cold biscuit.

Had Jeremiah eaten anything before going outside? What did he usually eat for breakfast? Was he satisfied with a cup of coffee and a biscuit or did he like bacon and eggs or flapjacks with syrup?

She washed down the last of her biscuit and jam with a swallow of coffee, set her cup in the sink, then walked to the window to look outside. What had kept him so long in the barn? Was he avoiding her as he had last night? For a moment, she considered putting on her coat and going out to join him, but in the end, she decided against it. If he wanted to be with her, he knew where she'd be.

I'll be patient. I must be patient. I love him. That's enough for now.

Drawing a breath, she turned to face the living area.

This was her home. She was Mrs. Jeremiah West, the mistress of the house. Therefore, she would begin to live that way.

Sarah spent the next hour or so acquainting herself with every nook and cranny of the log house, cleaning as she went. She counted the pots and pans and dishes and added to the list of items needed from the mercantile. She noted how many blankets they had and that they were in need of more sheets. She climbed the ladder to the loft, finding it full of dust and cobwebs but nothing else. The most notable thing about the house, in her mind, was the lack of anything that said a family lived there. It was plain, simple—and completely lacking in warmth. The necessities were provided for, but that was all.

Late in the morning, as she swept dust from beneath Jeremiah's bed, she found a small metal box. She pulled it into the open, wiping more dust from its top. Curious what this man—her new husband—might keep tucked away, she opened the lid.

Inside, there were several letters bound by a piece of string along with the deed to the West land. Beneath them, she found two photographs, and she felt a sting of guilt for looking at them. But she didn't put them back and close the lid.

Instead, she lifted the first photograph from the box. It was of a young man and woman on what appeared to be their wedding day. She wouldn't have recognized the groom as Ted West, except for his striking resemblance to Warren. The woman was small and delicate with dark eyes that were very much like Jeremiah's.

The second photograph had been taken near the lumber mill in Boulder Creek. Ted West stood in the middle, Jeremiah to his right, Warren to his left. She guessed Jeremiah would have been about fourteen. Almost a man and yet still a boy. He stood several inches taller than his father by that time. But what was most striking about the photograph was the distance between each member of the family. They stood apart from each other. She sensed the separation was even more emotional than physical. Sadness squeezed her heart.

"You don't have to be alone, Jeremiah," she whispered. "I'm here."

With a sigh, she returned the photographs to the box, closed the lid, and slid it under the bed before getting to her feet.

"How do I make you open up to me?"

She already loved him. Now she wanted to know him, to understand him.

Jeremiah West was a complicated man. She knew he cared for her, but he held so much back. If he wouldn't talk to her, how could she ever know what he held back? Or why.

She left the bedroom and walked to the window once again, staring in the direction of the barn, looking for any signs of her husband. At just that moment, he left the barn and walked toward the house, his hands in the pockets of his coat, his head bent forward against a winter wind. Rather than be caught looking for him, she went to the kitchen where she filled a cup with coffee, turning from the stove as the door opened.

JEREMIAH'S GAZE FOUND SARAH THE MOMENT HE ENTERED THE HOUSE. She wore a yellow calico today, and he was reminded of a meadow filled with wildflowers, bathed in a shower of sunshine. A sharp contrast to the wintery world beyond the door.

She held out a cup toward him. "You must be cold after all this time. Here. This coffee will warm you." She brought the drink to him. Her smile was tentative as he took the cup. After a moment, she turned away. "I've been thinking, Jeremiah." She filled a second cup with coffee from the speckled pot on the stove. "I don't know much about farming, but since I'm a farmer's wife now, I should learn." She turned to face him. "Shouldn't I?"

He tried to imagine her working in the fields with him, walking behind a plow or planting seeds. He failed to picture it in his mind. Her last name may have changed from McNeal to West, but she still belonged in some fancy parlor, pouring tea from a delicate teapot.

"And I know you weren't planning on marrying and having to worry about food and clothes for more than yourself. I want to help out that way, too."

He sat on the nearest chair.

His silence didn't seem to bother her, for she kept right on. "I didn't see a coop outside, but if you'd build one, I can take care of chickens for laying and some for eating. We could have all the eggs we wanted and sell the extra ones to the mercantile. Ralph Evans has chickens he sells. I went to school with his wife, Belle, and she told me they've got some of the finest laying hens in the entire state. I'm sure Belle would show me how to care for them."

Her bravery and determination were hard to resist. He could afford to buy some chickens. There was enough lumber behind the barn to build a fair-sized coop, and he could get whatever else he needed in town.

"And another thing. I'm a good seamstress. I've made my own dresses since I was a girl." She touched her yellow skirt. "I made this one."

"It's pretty." *You're pretty.*

"I could even offer my services to Mrs. Gaunt for alterations and such if—"

"You don't need to work for Mrs. Gaunt."

"But I—"

"No." He looked away, turning his gaze out the window. He wanted to take care of Sarah. He'd promised to take care of her. He would succeed as a farmer. He wouldn't fail her. "You won't need to take in sewing for others for us to get by." Drawing in a deep breath, he hoped what he said was true.

Her hand touched his knee, drawing his gaze, surprised she'd come so close without him hearing her approach. "I never doubted you'd take care of me. I never doubted it for a minute."

Perhaps Sarah didn't doubt it, but he did. He couldn't seem to help doubting. She didn't know how many times he'd failed the people who'd mattered to him.

But he knew.

CHAPTER

TWENTY-NINE

A warm wind blew in from the west during the following night, and when Sarah awakened in the morning, it was to the rhythmic sound of melting snow dripping off the roof. At least she hadn't slept late again. The sky outside her window was still dark as ink.

Tossing aside the blankets, she rose and went to the wash basin. The wood floor felt cold beneath her bare feet, and she didn't dawdle with her ablutions, especially since the water in the pitcher was as cold as the floor. Fully awake now, she dressed, then brushed her hair and captured it into a bun at her nape.

When she exited the bedroom a short while later, she discovered Jeremiah in the kitchen. Her pulse quickened, and a soft gasp of surprise escaped her throat.

He turned from the stove, coffee in hand. "Morning." He offered a brief smile. "Are you up for a trip into town today?"

The flutter in her heart had more to do with his smile than with the offer of going to town.

"I need to get my saddle horse from the livery, and you mentioned we needed some supplies from the mercantile."

"How soon do you want to go?"

"After breakfast, I suppose."

She felt a flush rise in her cheeks. He must think her spoiled and pampered, always the last to rise. "Of course. I'll prepare something right away."

"There's no hurry, Sarah. It's still early."

His gentle tone soothed her embarrassment.

"I'll feed the horse so he'll be ready when we are."

A COUPLE OF HOURS LATER, SARAH AND JEREMIAH SET OFF FOR Boulder Creek in the sleigh.

Trees stood bare, like gray skeletons, the snow that had blanketed them melted overnight. Sarah knew winter wasn't over, but when spring came, the stands of cottonwood and aspen would drape themselves in lush green robes, and from their branches, birds would welcome each day with song.

She closed her eyes, allowing her imagination to see the passing countryside as it would be as the seasons changed.

In the spring, pastures would roll with long grasses waving in the fresh breeze. Farmers would turn their fields, and the air would be filled with the earthy scent of rich, dark soil awaiting planting. In the summer, the days would turn hot. Wildflowers in glorious shades of yellow, purple, blue, and white would spill across the valley like an overturned jar of jelly beans on the mercantile floor. Morning glories would crawl along the ground and climb banisters on front porches. By September, the days would cool, the nights would turn cold. Dust would roll in giant clouds behind wagons and buggies as they went to and from town, and the scents of autumn would replace those of the spring and summer.

"We're here," Jeremiah said, interrupting her pleasant musings.

She was surprised to find they were in town already.

"Nervous?" he asked.

"About what?"

"They're probably still gossiping about our wedding."

She gave a slight shrug. "There's always gossip in a small town." Gathering her courage, she slipped her hand into the crook of his arm. Would he mind? She held on anyway.

He covered her hand with one of his and met her gaze. "I'll be beside you if you need me."

I do need you. I wish you knew how much.

Jeremiah guided the horse and sleigh to the mercantile. After stopping, he wrapped the reins around the brake handle before he hopped down from the seat, landing in a couple of inches of slush. He grimaced, knowing his feet would be plenty cold before he could dry them by the fire at home.

He walked around to the opposite side of the sleigh. Sarah stood and he took hold of her, both hands on her waist, and lifted her through the air to the boardwalk. A surprised laugh trailed behind her. The sound made him grin.

"I wasn't expecting that." She looked at him, eyes sparkling.

Her delight warmed him more than a fire would. "I didn't want your shoes to get wet."

"You're always thoughtful, Jeremiah."

"Not always."

She reached up with a gloved hand, touching his face. "Always with me."

Clearing his throat, he turned, his right hand against the small of her back. Together they entered the store.

Before the door closed behind them, Leslie Blake welcomed them. "Land o' Goshen! George, look who's here. It's Mr. and Mrs. West." She bustled from behind the counter, her arms outstretched. "You sure gave everyone a surprise, marrying the way you did." She hugged Sarah, then stepped back to look at Jeremiah. "Quite a surprise."

He forced a smile. "Marrying without a fuss seemed like the right thing to do."

George came out of the stockroom. "Up until Sunday, Sarah was the prettiest single gal in three counties, and don't think the young bucks hereabouts didn't know it." He shook Jeremiah's hand with an iron grip. "Come the spring thaw, there'd have been a herd of them hanging about the McNeal house." He released Jeremiah's hand and looked at Sarah. "I wish you a world of happiness. Both of you."

"Thank you," she said.

Seeing her smile, Jeremiah felt breathless. The desire to hold her close, to kiss her lips, swept through him like a prairie fire, and his heart pounded against his ribs.

"Well, what can we do for you?" Leslie asked.

The question doused the dangerous direction of his thoughts.

Sarah drew a slip of paper from the pocket of her skirt. "We need these supplies."

"'Course you do. Jeremiah hasn't purchased enough since he got here to see to a body's need. It's a wonder you both didn't plum starve in the last two days." Leslie took hold of Sarah's arm and led her away from the men.

George patted Jeremiah on the back. "You're a lucky man. A very lucky man."

"Yes, I am."

SARAH FINGERED THE FLANNEL FABRIC, THINKING IT WOULD BE perfect for a shirt for Jeremiah. She could make it for him as a surprise. Would he like that? Did he like surprises or did he prefer to plan ahead?

"Good day, Mrs. Bonnell," Leslie said. "I'll be with you in a moment."

Sarah felt a sinking sensation in the pit of her stomach. Ethel Bonnell, the town busybody, had never seemed to like her. Whenever Jeremiah or others used the word gossip, it was Ethel's face that appeared in Sarah's mind.

"My goodness! Sarah McNeal, is that you?"

Taking a deep breath to steel herself, she turned around. "Good morning, Mrs. Bonnell."

"I thought that was your grandfather's sleigh I saw outside, but I didn't expect to find you in town."

"Yes, it's Grandpa's sleigh."

"Such a surprise you gave everyone, getting married without a word to a soul. And to Jeremiah West, of all people."

"It's the way we wanted it. Just the two of us and family."

Ethel's eyes had the gleam of a predator. "Such a shame the groom's family couldn't be there, too." She raised a hand to cover her mouth. "I'm sorry. What a careless thing to say. Naturally, Warren wouldn't have wanted to be there, given the circumstances."

"What circumstances are those?" Jeremiah stepped out of the stockroom, his expression hard.

Ethel's eyes widened as she turned. "Mr. West, I didn't know you were there."

"Obviously." He moved to Sarah's side. "You were saying? About circumstances."

Her color high, Ethel took a step back. "Well, certainly everyone knows... Everyone thinks..." She drew herself up, nose tilted in the air. "She *was* engaged to Warren until you showed up in Boulder Creek."

"Sarah broke her engagement to my brother a month before she and I decided to marry. My wife was under no obligation to him or anyone else." The tone of his voice dared the woman to say another word.

Sarah's heart fluttered. A smile pulled at the corners of her mouth. Had Ethel Bonnell ever been put in her place like that before? Especially by a man. Doubtful.

Jeremiah glanced toward the counter. "Mrs. Blake, is our order ready?"

"Yes." Leslie tried to hide her own smile behind her hand. "Yes, it is."

"Good." He returned his gaze to Sarah. "It's time we went to your grandfather's."

He loves me. The certainty of it caused a thrill of delight to shoot through Sarah. *He may not know it yet, but he does love me.*

He met her gaze. "I'll put the supplies in the sleigh. Won't take me long."

As her husband walked away, Sarah glanced at Ethel, her smile growing. She didn't care what that woman thought of her, as long as she knew Jeremiah cared. "Good day, Mrs. Bonnell." Winking at Leslie, she slid the bolt of fabric back into its place on the shelf before following Jeremiah out the door.

THIRTY

Fifteen minutes later, as Jeremiah pulled back on the reins, stopping the horse in front of the McNeal house, surprise tingled inside Sarah's chest. This house had been her home for as long as she could remember. She'd loved her room. She'd loved the familiar kitchen. She'd loved the many mealtimes spent around the large dining room table. But it no longer felt like home. She'd been married only two days, and already she knew that her true home was a house made of logs located in the valley outside of Boulder Creek. It was a small house with an unadorned living area and a simple kitchen and two small bedrooms. It had a front stoop rather than a porch. In addition to the house, there was a large barn and a corral, and beneath the blanket of snow lay land that would grow crops come the summer sun.

"Sarah?"

She turned to look at Jeremiah who now stood beside the sleigh, offering his hand to help her down. "Sorry," she said. "I was lost in thought."

"I could tell." Humor laced his words.

It pleased her that his anger at Ethel Bonnell hadn't lasted long. It revealed one more good thing about his character. She took hold of his hand and stepped to the ground.

"Hey, Sarah!"

She looked in the direction of Tom's voice.

"This is a surprise."

"We came into town for more supplies."

Tom came down the walkway to the gate. "I'm headed over to Doc Varney's."

"Is Grandpa inside?"

"Yes. Will you stay long?"

She glanced at Jeremiah who gave a small shrug. "Not long," she answered her brother. "Perhaps an hour."

He leaned close and kissed her cheek. "I'll be back before you leave. I've got something to tell you."

"Something to tell me? What?"

Rather than answer, Tom grinned and took off in the direction of the doctor's house.

She looked at Jeremiah. "What do you suppose that was about?"

"Don't know." He cupped her elbow. "Let's go see your grandfather."

Inside, they found Grandpa seated in the overstuffed chair near the fireplace, an open book in his lap, his reading glasses perched on the end of his nose, his eyes closed. Sarah put an index finger to her lips, then moved across the room where she leaned forward and kissed his forehead.

"Hmm." He blinked. "What—"

"Hello, Grandpa."

"Princess." He sat up straight in the chair. "I didn't expect to see you until Sunday."

"No one does, apparently." She knelt on the floor and took hold of his hands. "How are you feeling?"

"Like I'm older than I want to be. Question is, how're you?"

"I'm fine. I'm happy."

Her grandfather's gray eyes searched her face. "Yes, I think you are." He glanced over Sarah's head. "Hello, Jeremiah."

"Sheriff McNeal."

"You decided what you're gonna do?"

Wondering what her grandfather meant, Sarah looked over her shoulder.

"I've given it some thought, sir. I need a job, at least until I can bring in my first crop, but I'm not sure how much good I'll be as a deputy, living so far out in the valley. If I was working at the sawmill like my dad did, it wouldn't matter. Nobody needs lumber in the middle of the night. Same can't be said about a deputy."

"No...no, it can't."

"I'm willing to come into town during the day if that'll suit you." His gaze dropped to Sarah. "But I'll spend my nights at the farm. With my wife."

A warm sensation coiled in her belly. She wanted to rise and throw herself into his arms. It didn't matter that he had yet to admit his feelings. It didn't matter that he wanted to keep her at arm's-length. She saw his heart.

"Good thing I'm still capable of whatever comes up at night in this town until it's time for a new sheriff to take over. So, Deputy West, I'll see you back at work next Monday."

"I'll be there, sir."

Still basking in Jeremiah's expression of care—although he might not have meant to reveal what he felt—Sarah listened as he excused himself to go get his saddle horse. Then she was alone with her grandfather.

"It's good to see you happy," Grandpa said.

"Yes." She smiled. "I love him."

Those three words didn't seem enough to express what she

felt. How could she explain? When she was with Jeremiah, she was whole, complete. The sun was brighter. The air was sweeter. No, he hadn't said he loved her. No, he hadn't taken her yet to their marriage bed. But still, she had hope, and she was happy. For now it was enough.

"I understand, princess."

Looking into her grandfather's eyes, she thought perhaps he did.

AFTER LEAVING THE LIVERY, JEREMIAH RODE TO THE SHERIFF'S OFFICE. He tethered his buckskin to the hitching post, then climbed the steps leading to the storage room above the jail. Strange, the room seemed smaller and bleaker than he remembered. In comparison, the farmhouse now seemed bigger and brighter than ever.

Because of Sarah.

He sat on the cot.

He loved her. He'd tried not to love her, but he'd failed in that, too. He loved her. She'd moved into his heart with the swift determination of a cavalry charge.

"But it changes nothing," he whispered. He closed his eyes and envisioned Sarah. "God, help me." He covered his face with his hands.

He'd proposed marriage, saying he wanted to protect her. But that wasn't his real reason. He'd wanted her with him. He'd wanted her for himself. She'd made him feel whole again, and he hadn't wanted to risk losing that. Selfishly, he'd wanted to be with her forever, even before he'd loved her.

"How do I fix this?"

Silence met him. A deep silence.

He could go. He could leave Boulder Creek. His horse

waited for him outside. He could mount up and ride away. Ride south. Ride north. It didn't matter where. He'd wandered for years. He could wander again.

But he wouldn't go. He wouldn't leave Sarah. He couldn't do that to her. He couldn't do that to himself.

Sarah leaned close to the dining room window, looking south toward the center of town. There was no sign of her husband or his horse on the street.

"I wonder what's keeping him," she whispered.

As she stepped back from the glass, she saw Tom walking toward the house from a different direction. At least she wouldn't have to wait much longer to learn what news her brother wanted to tell her.

"Tom's back," she called to her grandfather as she moved to the entry hall.

Tom grinned when he saw her waiting for him. "Glad you're still here. I was afraid I took too long at Doc's."

"I'm waiting for Jeremiah. He went to get his horse at the livery."

"Well, then. Let's talk." He motioned with his head toward the kitchen. "I could use something hot to drink."

"Tea?"

"If there's no coffee."

"There isn't. I washed the pot myself a little while ago."

"Tea then."

"See if Grandpa wants any," Sarah said as she headed for the kitchen. Unlike Jeremiah's house—her new home—she knew where everything was here. In short order, she'd filled the kettle with water and set it on the stove to heat. Then she took the canister of tea from one cupboard to wait on the counter beside three cups.

"No tea for Grandpa." Tom entered the kitchen and stood near the stove. "He's asleep in his chair. Sound asleep."

The third cup went back onto the shelf.

"Sarah." Her brother cleared his throat. "I've met somebody."

The kettle began to whistle, and she reached for it. "Somebody new to town?"

"Not exactly."

About to pour hot water into the cups, she paused to look at Tom.

"I've met a girl. Someone special." His expression said much more than his words.

Sarah returned the kettle to the stove. "Who?"

"Fanny. Fanny Adams."

She gave her head a slow shake, not recognizing the name.

"She came to Boulder Creek early last summer. She works at the boarding house now. Stays there, too." Tom took charge of the tea-making. "I met her when...when Doc was called to see to her."

"She was sick?"

"Not exactly."

Sarah frowned at the repeated phrase. Why was he being evasive? He was the one who'd wanted to tell her about this girl he'd met.

"Sis, I think I'm falling in love."

She straightened in surprise. "Tom, you're only eighteen."

"I know how old I am."

"How old is she?"

"Seventeen."

"Where did she come from?"

"Up north."

Sarah pushed a stray lock of hair away from her face. She didn't remember seeing an unfamiliar girl coming or going from Virginia Tomkin's boarding house in recent months. She wasn't anyone who'd attended Reverend Jacobs's church. But maybe this Miss Adams was a member of the Methodist Church at the other end of town. Still, Boulder Creek was small. How could she not have met her in all these months?

Giving her head a slight shake, she said, "Tom, you leave in a couple of months for school."

"I know that."

"This is no time for a romance. You're studying to be a doctor."

"I know that too." There was an edge in his voice now. It announced that stubborn trait that ran through all the McNeals.

A sigh escaped her. There was no point making a big deal of this. Her brother was young. He might forget the girl even before he left Boulder Creek, and he most surely would once he was back in school, training to be a doctor.

"I figured you of all people would understand what it's like, falling for somebody so fast. The way you love Jeremiah."

She looked at her brother in surprise. He'd certainly changed his tune from only two days ago. He'd sounded skeptical on her wedding day.

Before either of them could say more, the front door opened. Sarah looked through the kitchen doorway to see Jeremiah entering the house. His gaze met hers, and he gave her a quick smile. Her heart fluttered in response.

"Sorry it took me so long," he said.

"No matter."

"We'd better go. Night falls fast."

"I'm ready." She looked at Tom. "We'll see you on Sunday. We'll talk more then."

THIRTY-ONE

S arah awakened the next morning, a dream lingering at the edges of her memory. In only a moment or two, it was gone, all except for the image of Jeremiah smiling at her. That remained, and it seemed to take the chill from her still dark bedroom.

Something had changed between them yesterday. She'd felt it in his posture during the ride home in the sleigh. She'd seen it in his glances across the supper table. She'd heard it in his voice when he'd bid her goodnight.

Jeremiah had softened toward her in a way she couldn't define, but she knew it all the same.

Hope blossoming in a new way in her heart, she pushed aside the blankets and rose from bed. The cold morning air hurried her through her preparations for the day. Minutes later, with her hair captured with a ribbon at the nape, she left the bedroom, oil lamp in hand. This time, Jeremiah's bedroom door was still closed. She'd managed to rise before him.

With quick efficiency, she got a fire burning in the cook stove and prepared the coffee. When water in the pot was starting to heat, she went to the stove in the living room and soon had a fire burning there too. Before long, its heat was chasing the cold into the far corners of the room.

"Morning, Sarah."

Startled by the sound of Jeremiah's voice, she turned toward his bedroom door. His tall frame filled most of the space. "Good morning." Warmth spread through her. Warmth that had nothing to do with the nearby stove.

"You're up early." He raked the fingers of one hand through his hair, mussing it.

She ignored the comment and asked, "Are you hungry? I can fix your breakfast."

"I'll tend to the horses first. Then I'll be ready to eat." A smile tugged at one corner of his mouth. "I won't be long."

She watched him put on his coat and leave through the front door, then she returned to the kitchen and got ready to make his breakfast the moment he returned.

A snippet of that morning's dream came to mind: Jeremiah smiling before he bent low to kiss her. Her pulse jumped and sped, and she sank onto a chair, her hand touching her lips, as if to capture that envisioned kiss.

Lost in thought, she was caught by surprise when the door opened, announcing Jeremiah's return. She rose and went to the stove, unable to look at him, afraid he would see the longing in her eyes.

"Thought I'd try to finish that chicken coop when it warms up a bit," he said. "Might even have time today to ride over to the Evans place to buy some of his laying hens. Maybe a rooster too."

"Finish it?" She glanced over her shoulder. "I didn't know you'd started." She'd only made mention of a chicken coop two days ago.

"Got some work done on it yesterday after we returned

from town. I bought the last of the things I needed when we were there."

He'd done it for her. He'd done so much for her. Big things. Little things. Loving things. If she knew that he loved her, why wasn't he able to admit it? Somehow she had to help him let go of whatever held him back.

THE RUNNERS ON THE SLEIGH MADE A *SWOOSHING* SOUND AS THEY SLID over the snow, and the horse's pace quickened as they drew closer to a warm barn with hay in the manger.

Behind Jeremiah, a wood crate held six chickens. Their raucous squawking told him they weren't happy with this cold journey. Beside him on the seat, a black and white puppy snuggled deep in the folds of a blanket.

"What do you suppose Sarah will have to say about you?" Jeremiah asked aloud as he stroked the puppy's head with gloved fingers.

He grinned, knowing the answer. She would love it. She would spoil it. She would be delighted that he'd gone to get chickens and had come home with chickens and a puppy too.

"You'd better turn out to be smart. You'll have to work the farm along with us."

Us.

Jeremiah and Sarah.

We.

Two made one. In all ways but one.

He pushed the thought aside as the house came into view, smoke curling above the chimneys. Easing back on the reins, he slowed the horse to a walk.

Home. He was home. It wasn't home because he lived there. It wasn't home because he'd been raised there. Because he'd inherited it. It was home because Sarah waited there for him.

As if summoned by his thoughts, the door opened, and Sarah stepped outside, a shawl pulled tight around her shoulders. She smiled and waved, and he couldn't help but do the same in return.

"You got the chickens?" She ran after the sleigh as he drove to the barn.

"I got them." He hopped down from the seat and reached for the crate.

The chickens voiced their displeasure.

"Oh, look at them. Poor things. They must be cold."

He set the crate on the ground and turned back to the wagon seat. "I've got something else that's cold." He faced Sarah, blanket held close to his chest.

She gave him a puzzled look.

The puppy's head popped from beneath the folds of the blanket.

"Oh, Jeremiah. A puppy."

"He's yours."

"Mine?"

"Well, yours to train. He'll have plenty to learn as he gets older. Including how to keep foxes and other critters out of the chicken coop."

She rubbed the puppy's head against her cheek. "He's adorable."

Adorable. The exact word he would have used to describe Sarah.

Clearing his throat, he picked up the crate and carried it toward the newly constructed coop on the south side of the barn. Minutes later, the chickens getting acquainted with their new home, Jeremiah turned toward the horse and sleigh. His eyes widened when he saw Sarah releasing the horse from its traces. He hadn't thought she would know how.

He hurried to the barn door and opened it, allowing Sarah to lead the horse inside. He looked for the puppy, but couldn't find it. "Where's the—?" he began.

Sarah glanced down. The puppy stared back at Jeremiah from the pocket of her skirt.

He laughed. "Good thing he isn't any bigger."

"Isn't it?" She laughed too.

He didn't know how it happened. All he knew for sure is that one step took him close enough to draw Sarah into his arms. He stared down into her eyes, the blue depths turned dark gray in the dim light of the barn. Then he drew her close and kissed her. Kissed her as he hadn't allowed himself to kiss her before. As he shouldn't allow himself to kiss her now.

A soft groan sounded in her throat, causing desire to flare within him.

He broke the kiss and stepped back. "I'm sorry."

"Don't be sorry. Jeremiah, I—"

"You should get back inside. That shawl's not enough to keep you warm."

"Please don't push me away."

"Sarah..."

She laid the flat of her hand against his chest. "Please don't push me away."

"Sarah, you don't understand."

"Isn't there room for me in your heart?" Her voice was soft and low, yet the question seemed loud.

She had no clue. She'd already taken up residence in his heart.

She moved her hand from his chest to the side of his face. He closed his eyes, only for an instant, and leaned into it.

"I love you, Jeremiah."

His eyes opened. He heard his dad saying he wouldn't amount to anything. He remembered Marta's last moments of life, the doctor coming too late, and recalled the promises he'd made that the same would never happen to Sarah. But it wasn't enough. It wasn't nearly enough.

He drew her back into his arms and told her with his kisses what he wouldn't let himself put into words.

CHAPTER

THIRTY-TWO

For Sarah, the month of February passed in a glow of contentment. While her husband spent most days in town, working as the deputy, she continued to turn the old farmhouse into a real home. She made curtains for the windows. She worked on a quilt for the bed she now shared with Jeremiah. She tended the chickens. And she did her best to keep Bandit, as they'd named the puppy, out of trouble.

Sundays after church with Grandpa and Tom seemed even more special than before. And since her brother never mentioned Fanny Adams to Sarah again, she assumed she'd been right not to worry about her. He'd forgotten the girl already. Now he could prepare to leave for school without anything clouding his judgment.

The only shadow on Sarah's happiness was Jeremiah's refusal to say the words she most longed to hear—that he loved her. When he looked at her, when he touched her, when he kissed her, she knew the depths of his feelings. So why was he unwilling to speak them aloud? What kept the words locked inside his heart? She wanted to understand but couldn't.

She was pondering those questions once again one afternoon in early March when she heard the rattle of a wagon entering the yard. She set her sewing aside and went to the door, opening it to find Addie Danson stepping down from the wagon seat. A thin layer of mud splashed onto Addie's skirt and sucked at her boots.

"Mrs. Danson, this is a surprise."

Addie smiled. "With most of the snow gone, I thought it was time I came calling. Is your husband around?"

"No, Jeremiah's in town today."

"Well, I guess I'll leave my wedding gift with you."

"A gift? But you shouldn't—"

"What do you think of her?" Addie motioned toward the horse tied to the back of the wagon. "She's yours. Yours and Jeremiah's."

Sarah couldn't believe it. The mare was a beautiful sorrel with a flaxen mane and tail. Her coat gleamed with reddish highlights in the afternoon sunlight.

"She'll give you a grand foal before long."

"Mrs. Danson, we couldn't possibly accept such a valuable gift."

"I want you to have her, Sarah." Addie shortened the distance between them. "If you've got a moment to spare, I'll share something with you."

"Of course. Do come in." She backed up and held the door open wide.

After Addie had cleaned the mud from her boots to keep from tracking up the floor and Sarah had made them both some tea, the two women sat across from each other at the table.

"You've been busy," Addie said. "This house never looked this way when Ted West was alive. You've brought a warmth to it."

"Thank you." Sarah glanced toward the window. "Mrs. Danson, about the mare, we can't—"

"Please, Sarah. It's my way of paying a debt."

"A debt?"

"You were a toddler when I moved to Boulder Creek from Connecticut to be the town's first teacher. I was homesick at first, but then I fell in love with Will Danson." Her expression turned dreamy, making her look much younger than her actual age. Like a schoolgirl herself. "After I accepted his proposal, your mother offered me the use of her wedding gown. I'll never forget the day she showed it to me. Cream silk faille, cotton sateen, and Belgian lace. I felt like a storybook princess when I tried it on."

"I've seen the photographs of my parents' wedding day. The dress was beautiful."

"Photographs can't do it justice."

"I wish I could have seen it myself. It was ruined that summer we had so much flooding."

A frown replaced the wistful expression. "I'd forgotten that. A real shame." Addie shook her head. "Anyway, I never got a chance to thank your mother properly. Tom was born about an hour or so after the minister pronounced Will and me man and wife." She looked down at her teacup.

Sarah knew what the woman hadn't said. Maria McNeal had died that day, not long after giving birth to Sarah's brother.

"So, you see," Addie continued, "this is my way of saying thank you to your mother all these years later. Please. Don't refuse my gift."

Sarah nodded, finding it impossible to speak around the lump in her throat.

"Good. Now, you put on your wrap and come out and have

a closer look at her. The Rocking D raises the finest horses in the whole state, and Ember is no exception."

"Ember?"

"My youngest named her. You remember Naomi. She thought this mare's coloring looked like embers in the fireplace. The name stuck."

"Ember. I like it."

The two women rose and went outside. As they rounded the end of the wagon, Sarah saw the mare's swollen belly and knew Addie hadn't exaggerated when she'd said it wouldn't be long before the horse gave birth.

"Ember's the granddaughter of the mare I bought from Will when I first came to Boulder Creek. Close to twenty years ago, that was."

"Are you sure you want to—"

"I'm sure. Now, let's take her into that barn of yours and get her settled." She untied the rope from the wagon, then led the mare across the barnyard.

Sarah's grandparents had given her a horse when she was a girl. Victoria, named for the Queen of England, had been old and not much to look at, but Sarah had loved her all the same. In the summer, she'd ridden the mare off by herself where she could sit and dream about the places she wanted to go, the things she wanted to see. Now she and Jeremiah owned not only this beautiful mare, but they would soon have a foal to raise. Blessing upon blessing.

As they entered the barn, Jeremiah's new work horse thrust his big, black head over the stall rail and nickered to the newcomer. Ember answered with a nicker of her own.

Addie selected one of the two empty stalls and led the mare inside. "I suspect she'll drop her foal in another week or two. Jeremiah knows what to do when her time comes. He's got good sense when it comes to horses."

"How do you know?"

"He worked for Will one summer as a boy." Addie removed the halter, then scratched the mare behind one ear. Ember bobbed her head up and down in pleasure.

I wish I'd known Jeremiah back then.

"You've married a good man, Sarah."

She met Addie's gaze. "I know."

"And he's married a good woman."

She drew in a breath. "Thank you."

"He knows it too. It's written on his face whenever the two of you are together." Addie offered a smile of encouragement. "The gossip is nearly over. Go right on paying no mind to it. Most folks know it's nonsense."

"Thank you," she said again, the words a whisper this time.

Addie stepped near and put an arm around Sarah's shoulders. "You and Jeremiah were meant to be together. Trust me. I have a nose for such things."

Sarah wished she could ask Addie the questions that swirled inside of her. What had Jeremiah been like as a boy? What was Marta like? Why had those two fallen in love back then? Why couldn't Jeremiah express his love today?

But she couldn't ask. One day, perhaps. But not now.

JEREMIAH STROLLED ALONG THE BOARDWALK, TOUCHING THE BRIM OF his calvary hat as he nodded to townsfolk. Spring-like temperatures had brought people out of their homes and into town. The warmer weather had also made the ground muddy, creating less than desirable walking conditions. That wouldn't last long. Another cold snap—weeks of it—would freeze it all again.

But eventually, the snow would be gone. The earth would

warm, and the soil would be ready to turn and plant. His hands itched to hold the plow again. It was what he'd returned to Boulder Creek to do.

He thought of Sarah, out in the barnyard, feeding her chickens, the sun catching the golden highlights in her hair. He imagined her hanging laundry to dry as wildflowers bloomed on the hillsides. He pictured her beside him—

Loud laughter brought him out of his reverie. Six men walked toward him. Strangers with long and shaggy hair, their faces bearded, their clothes unwashed. One man slapped another on the back and shouted a rude expletive at the fellow behind him. The leader of the group pushed open the slatted doors of the saloon and they disappeared inside. The others followed.

"Spring's about here."

He turned toward Hank McNeal's voice. The sheriff stood just outside the entrance to Zoe's Restaurant. "Who are they?"

"Loggers headed up to the camps. They got off the train from Boise today. There'll be plenty more coming through Boulder Creek for the next month or two. A steady stream of them. If there's trouble, it'll start in the saloon."

Jeremiah nodded.

Hank looked up at the clear sky. "Won't be long before you're able to put in your crops. I reckon you're eager to get started."

"I am."

"I've started looking to hire a new deputy." Hank released a breath. "And, since I plan to retire before the next election, the mayor will need to appoint my replacement soon."

"You're retiring?" He didn't know why he was surprised. The older man had mentioned his readiness to retire more than once since Jeremiah's return to Boulder Creek.

"Past time I did so."

"Do you know who'll take your place?"

"Could've been you if you'd wanted it."

Jeremiah huffed. "I don't."

"Too bad."

"It'll be a big change for you, not being sheriff."

In unspoken agreement, the two men began to walk toward the jail.

Hank said, "Not as much as you might think. You carried most of the weight over the winter. I've rather liked spending time by the fire, reading a book or taking a nap. I suppose I'll just do more of that. Especially after Tom leaves for school."

"You'll miss him when he's gone."

"I will, at that. The house'll seem empty. But you and Sarah aren't too far away, and I've got plenty of friends here in town. I'll get by well enough." Hank gave him a sideways glance. "And maybe you and Sarah will get around to making me a great-grandpa. It'd be nice to bounce a little one on these cantankerous old knees."

Fear iced through Jeremiah. He tried not to think of that possibility. He'd given into his desire for his bride, but that didn't change his hope that she wouldn't become pregnant. If he were to lose her because of his selfishness...

He could only hope God would strike him dead first.

A COLD DREAD PURSUED JEREMIAH ON THE WAY OUT OF TOWN THAT evening, Hank's words replaying in his mind: *"Maybe you and Sarah will get around to making me a great-grandpa."*

As he brought the buckskin to a halt near the barn, the door to the house opened and Sarah rushed out. Something was wrong. Something must be wrong. He'd felt it in his gut all day.

"You'll never guess what happened," she called, hurrying toward him.

It took a few moments for him to register her smile and the joy in her voice.

"Addie Danson came to call. She brought us a wedding gift."

He stepped down from the saddle, still uncertain.

"Wait until you see it." She took hold of his hand and tugged his arm.

"Let me put up my horse first."

"I'm taking you to the barn. That's where our gift is."

"In the barn?"

"Come on." She pulled on his arm again.

He went with her, leading the buckskin behind him.

"I couldn't believe it, Jeremiah. You won't either. Wait until you see."

His fear dissipated at last.

A few yards from the barn, Sarah dropped his hand and hurried forward to open the door. As he approached, she motioned him inside. At first, he saw nothing out of the ordinary. The work horse he'd purchased from Chad Turner's livery thrust his head over the stall railing and snorted as he bobbed his head. It was the way the big black welcomed Jeremiah and the buckskin back from town every day. Then another horse head appeared out of what, that morning, had been an empty stall. Jeremiah stopped and stared before glancing over his shoulder at Sarah.

"Isn't she wonderful?" Her smile was even brighter than before. "Her name's Ember, and she's going to give us a foal in a week or two."

He moved to the edge of the stall for a better look. He noted the mare's fine conformation, evident despite her swollen belly. "This isn't a ten dollar saddle horse. Why would the Dansons give us such a gift?"

"Because of a debt Addie Danson believes she owed my mother." Sarah stepped up beside him. "She said you've got good sense when it comes to horses. She told me you worked at their ranch one spring."

"Yes."

"Tell me about it."

Jeremiah smiled to himself. How often did Sarah say those words to him? *Tell me about it.* She wanted to know him, everything about him. If only he could give her what she wanted.

He reached out and touched her cheek with his fingertips, then flattened his palm against the side of her face. She tipped her head to the side, pressing closer.

Trust.

Strange, the way that single word seemed to speak volumes more.

He needed to trust. To trust Sarah. To trust God. Perhaps even to trust himself.

Could he do that?

He wanted to do that.

THIRTY-THREE

Four days later, Sarah listened to the sounds of Jeremiah working outside while she prepared their lunch. The saw ground and screeched as it cut through lumber, and a short while later, the rhythmic smack of the hammer drove nails into boards.

Maybe a time will come when we'll do more than repair the barn. Perhaps we'll need to add onto the house.

She lowered a hand to her abdomen, wishing for the day she might know she was with child.

Jeremiah's child. Perhaps a son.

She smiled. It was easy to imagine their little boy, toddling after his father, following him around the barnyard. He would have Jeremiah's dark hair, sooty eyes, and handsome smile.

Would Jeremiah be happy if she became pregnant? Her smile faded at the question. There were moments when she was sure of Jeremiah's feelings for her, unspoken though they were. There were others when she feared he might get on his horse and ride out of her life because she wanted too much from him. But why did he feel that way? Why was he afraid to love her?

The door opened behind her. "Hey, Sarah."

She turned.

"Ember's in labor."

She set down the knife and wiped her hands on her apron. "What do we need to do?"

"Nothing, if all goes well."

She removed her apron and laid it on the counter, then hurried toward the door where she retrieved her shawl from the peg.

"It could take a long time," he said. "Hours. I can call you when she's closer."

"No. I want to be there."

He grinned as he reached for her hand.

There was an air of expectation inside the barn. Sarah felt it the moment she entered alongside Jeremiah. Neither of the geldings whickered a greeting as they normally did. Even they seemed to know something out of the ordinary was about to happen.

Sarah went to the stall where Ember lay on her side, breathing labored. Once, the horse lifted her head and reached back to nip at her side.

"Is there anything we can do to help?" Sarah asked.

"No. Nature will take its course." He touched her shoulder. "Let's move away. Sometimes it makes a mare nervous to have humans too close."

He led the way to a shadowy corner and motioned for her to sit on a three-legged stool, then he sat nearby on an up-ended barrel. Sunlight spilled through the open doors in the hayloft and settled on the stall.

"Last time I did this was with Marta."

Sarah's pulse quickened, startled by his admission. He so

seldom spoke about the past. He almost never spoke about his first wife. At least not around Sarah.

"We lost that mare a few hours after she gave birth, but Marta managed to save the colt. She fixed up a bucket with a nipple and fed that foal day and night for weeks. Months, I guess." He drew a deep breath and released it. "I sold the colt after Marta died."

Sarah wished she could touch him, hold him, but she resisted the urge, afraid it would stop him from telling her about his life away from Boulder Creek.

"You would have liked Marta."

Tears pooled in her eyes.

"She was sixteen when we ran off. My dad was against us marrying. All my life, he'd told me I wouldn't amount to much, and he did his best to make sure I toed the line." He paused. "That was probably the angriest I ever saw my dad. He tried to tell me I couldn't ever see Marta again. He accused her of ruining my life." He drew in a deep breath. "We both said some mighty ugly things to each other that day."

Unable to stop herself any longer, Sarah touched his knee. He didn't seem to notice.

"I never should have taken her away from Boulder Creek. We didn't have much when we left. Just enough to get us to Ohio where her grandma lived. If it wasn't for Grandma Ashmore, we'd have starved before the first year was out. Just like my dad predicted."

Again he fell silent, and again she waited.

"Marta never complained. Not once in all those years we were in Ohio. No matter what she had to do without, she never complained. And she did without plenty."

"She loved you," Sarah whispered. "And you loved her."

"I never did right by her. I never took care of her the way I should've. The way I'd promised. I failed, like my dad said I would."

"Lots of people go through hard times, Jeremiah. It wasn't your fault. You were young. Both of you."

"Our baby was due any day when Marta took sick with a fever. We didn't have a doctor close by, and she said she'd be all right. I let her convince me that was true because we didn't have the money to pay for a doctor to come all that way. She was in a bad way already when she went into labor." He covered his face with his hands. "I waited too long before I sent for him. She'd still be alive if it wasn't for me."

"Oh, Jeremiah."

She'd known that Marta and their baby had died together, but until this moment, she hadn't understood what that loss had done to him. She hadn't understood the guilt he carried because of it.

"I failed, like my dad said I would."

"You can't know what would have happened," she said softly. "Only God knows what might have been."

He lowered his hands to look at her, devastation in the depths of his eyes.

"You can't know, Jeremiah." Pain squeezed her heart. "Perhaps the doctor couldn't have helped no matter how soon he arrived."

"Maybe. But I should have tried. I should have sent for him sooner. I should've done more."

"We can only do the best with what we have and who we are right at the moment." She leaned toward him. "You loved her. That was all she wanted from you." Silently she added, *It's all I want from you, too.*

He looked at her, perhaps seeing what she longed for. For a moment, she hoped—

Ember's squeal shattered the brief silence, causing them both to startle.

"The foal must be coming." Jeremiah stood and moved to the stall, leaving Sarah in the shadows.

For the first time since she'd agreed to marry him, she wondered if she might never hear him say he loved her. For the first time, her doubts were stronger than her hopes.

THAT NIGHT, LONG AFTER SARAH RETIRED, JEREMIAH SAT BY THE WOOD stove, lost in thought.

Ember's filly had arrived without trouble. It hadn't taken the foal long to rise on spindly legs, and it was obvious the little one would be the spitting image of her dam. A true beauty. He'd loved seeing Sarah's delight at the foal's birth, but he'd also seen a sadness in her eyes. A sadness he'd put there. He'd hurt her when he told her about his past. Perhaps she'd seen the way he'd failed Marta and realized he would fail her too.

He let his head droop forward, his eyes closed. "God, forgive me," he whispered.

In response, a Bible verse, one he'd learned as a boy, reverberated in his heart: *For the LORD thy God, he it is that doth go with thee; he will not fail thee, nor forsake thee.*

Jeremiah had failed often in his life. He'd failed in ways both large and small. But God hadn't failed him or forsaken him. The Lord had been beside him every step of the way, even when he'd walked through the valleys.

"You can't know what would have happened. Only God knows."

He straightened in the chair, and his gaze went to his mother's Bible. A memory teased him. He took the big book onto his lap and let it fall open. Then he began flipping through the pages. A long while later, he found the verse he sought.

And be not conformed to this world: but be ye transformed by the renewing of your mind, that ye may prove what is that good, and acceptable, and perfect, will of God.

He traced the words with his index finger. "Renew my mind," he whispered, lifting his eyes toward the bedroom. "I need to change the way I think." He lowered his gaze to the Bible again. "No. I am unable to do it. God, You need to change the way I think. I've tried and can't do it on my own."

Trust.

There was that word again. That call to trust. Sarah trusted God and she trusted him. Why couldn't he do the same? Why was it so difficult for him to let go of the past and live in the present?

"Help me, God."

THIRTY-FOUR

S arah felt the coolness of the sheets when she moved her feet toward the other side of the bed, and she knew Jeremiah had either risen early or he'd never come to bed at all.

Pushing aside the blankets, she sat up, fighting tears of disappointment and uncertainty. She'd felt such hope yesterday as Jeremiah led her into the barn to observe the arrival of Ember's foal. But by the time the filly was born, her hope had waned. It seemed to have vanished completely with the coming of this new day.

"What am I to do? How can I help him?"

When she left the bedroom, she found coffee prepared in the pot on the cook stove but Jeremiah wasn't in the house. She was about to go looking for him when she spied a slip of paper on the kitchen table.

Chad Turner starts his job as sheriff today. I'm riding into town early. Look for me before supper. J.

She ran her finger over his slanted handwriting on the paper as a sigh escaped her. She'd hoped to see Jeremiah before he left. Although what could she say that would make a difference?

"Nothing," she whispered.

With a shake of her head, she went to the door and put on her coat.

Outside, pale morning light blanketed the yard and barn. Patches of snow lingered in shady spots, but she knew it wouldn't last much longer. A few weeks at most. Even if another storm blew through the valley, as could happen in March and April, snow wouldn't last. Spring would have its way.

As was usual, she tended to the chickens first. After collecting eggs, she scattered feed for the hens and smiled as she watched their jerky movements and listened to their contented clucking. It felt familiar and comforting. In her mind, she imagined a toddler running about as she completed the chore. She seemed to hear the childish giggles. Oh, how she longed for that to become a reality.

Whispering a prayer for Jeremiah, she latched the gate on the chicken enclosure, then headed for the barn. Before she reached it, she heard Bandit's loud complaints. Jeremiah had insisted that a dog's place at night was in the barn. Sarah had acquiesced, but she didn't have to like it.

"I'm coming, Bandit." She pulled open the door.

The puppy's cries grew even louder as she approached the kennel. In moments, Sarah had set him free, and he jumped and bounced with joy, running circles around her.

"All right. All right. Be good now. Sit." She caught the puppy and pushed his rump onto the barn floor. The pup was quiet only until Sarah pulled her hand away. Immediately after, he was in action again. She laughed, her spirits lifting as she took Bandit into her arms. "This is the only way you'll be quiet."

She carried the pup over to Ember's stall. A quick glance told her that Jeremiah had fed and watered both Ember and the black before leaving for town.

"And what about you?" she asked the filly as it sidled closer to her dam. "Are you getting enough to eat?"

As if in answer, the foal thrust her muzzle under Ember, in search of an udder. As the filly suckled, Ember curved her neck to glance in her baby's direction, making sure she was safe and secure.

"Father," Sarah whispered, "You watch over Your children in the same way. Even in the storms, You keep us. Thank You for that." She drew a breath as her eyes closed and she rubbed her cheek against Bandit's head. "Help Jeremiah know that truth."

JEREMIAH AND CHAD TURNER BOTH STARTLED WHEN THE DOOR TO THE sheriff's office flew open, banging against the wall. Tom McNeal stood in the opening.

"Tom?" Jeremiah stood.

"Doc sent me. We've got trouble."

Chad, the newly-appointed sheriff, also stood. "At the saloon?"

"No, sir. We've got sickness. Six new cases this morning."

"Cases of what?" Jeremiah asked.

"Looks like influenza."

The word hit Jeremiah like a punch. Influenza had taken about a million lives around the world nine years before. The pandemic had started in Russia, so very far away, but it had found its way to a small house in Ohio and stolen the lives of his wife and baby.

"Doc tended to a couple of the loggers coming through

town last week. Looks like they were the first to take sick. Probably brought it here on the train. He says the school should be closed so we can send any patients there. The children need to stay home anyway to contain the spread. Some physicians don't think influenza is passed from person to person. They think it's a kind of miasma. Bad air carrying it around. But Doc disagrees. He says we've got to keep sick people away from healthy people. Quarantine is how we'll stop it."

Jeremiah nodded toward Tom, but what he wanted was to get on his horse and race for home.

Tom took a step back. "I'm headed over to tell the mayor what's happening. Then I need to get back to Doc's. Tell Sarah that I'll make sure Grandpa stays in the house and away from those who're sick."

"I'll tell her." Jeremiah turned toward Chad. "What do you want me to do?"

The sheriff rubbed his chin. "I never figured this was how my new job would start."

"I expected we might have trouble from the loggers. Never thought it would be because they were sick." Jeremiah reached for his coat.

Chad said, "I'll go to the school and send everyone home. You let folks in town know what's happening. Then we can make sure the news gets to the farmers and ranchers too."

The two men set about their individual tasks.

"First sign of fever or chills or a cough," Jeremiah told everyone in the general store and Zoe's Restaurant, "go to the school. Keep to yourselves."

He wasn't the only one who remembered the Russian Influenza. He saw dread in the faces of more than one person he spoke to as he made his way down one side of Main Street and then back along the other.

Jeremiah met the sheriff on the way back to the office.

Chad looked toward the saloon. Loud piano music and louder voices came through the open doors. "Doesn't sound like many of them are taking the warning seriously."

"No, sir. It doesn't."

Chad's gaze met Jeremiah's. "You oughta have time to spread the news to places west of town before you need to be home."

"All right."

"Wish I could tell you to just stay there." Again he looked toward the saloon. "But I have a feeling I may need you to help me keep order over the next few days."

Jeremiah nodded. God willing, it would only be a few days. *God, please be willing.*

ALTHOUGH THE TEMPERATURE REMAINED COOL, THE AFTERNOON SUN felt warm on Sarah's skin. Wearing a shawl around her shoulders, she stood in the yard, her face turned upward, her eyes closed. Throughout the day, she had prayed. Prayed for herself. Prayed for her husband. Prayed for their marriage. Prayed for the child she yearned for.

The fast clip of galloping hooves brought her eyes open moments before Jeremiah rode into view on his buckskin gelding. A frisson of alarm shot up her spine, then she leaned down to catch Bandit into her arms, hugging the puppy to her chest. The look on Jeremiah's face did nothing to soothe her as he brought the horse to a halt.

"What is it?"

He dropped to the ground, and she stepped toward him.

"Stay where you are, Sarah."

The abruptness of his tone more than his words caused her obedience. "What's happened?"

"There's sickness in town. It's serious. Looks like influenza."

"But—"

"I could get ill next. I've been around some who are."

"Who? Grandpa? Tom?"

He shook his head. "No. They're all right. Tom's working with Doc to take care of the sick." Pulling on the reins, he drew his horse around. "They're quarantining in the school. I'm going to put a few things together and go back to town. I'll sleep above the jail until this is over. Chad worries we might have trouble."

"He's new to the job," she said, stating the obvious. "He'll worry easily."

"I don't want you coming into town. Not until the sickness is gone. Not until there're no more patients for Doc to look after."

"Jeremiah, I can't—"

"You've got enough food here to get by."

"But I won't know what's happening. What if—"

"I'll send word." He took one step toward her. "I'll ride out every couple of days myself. But all I want right now is to know that you're safe."

She remembered Ember with her filly that morning. "Our Father is watching over us," she said softly. "I trust Him to care for me. And for you."

Surprise flickered in his eyes. And when it was gone, it took some of the fear with it. In its place, she saw love. Love for her.

Sarah offered a gentle smile. "Bandit and I will be fine. We'll care for the animals until you're back."

THIRTY-FIVE

The old and the young, Doc Varney had said, were at the most risk from this disease. And so it proved.

On Friday, Grace Richards, at eighty-seven, was the first to go. On Saturday, her two-year-old great-granddaughter and namesake, Gracie Frasier, succumbed to a high fever. Both were buried without fanfare.

A few days later—it seemed like an eternity—Jeremiah stood in the yard of the schoolhouse.

"We've got fifteen patients right now," Tom said in answer to Jeremiah's question. The young man looked like he hadn't slept in a year.

"Is there anything I can get you? Food. Anything."

Tom shook his head. "No, we're doing all right. Mrs. Varney's been bringing us food every day. And we've got a couple of volunteers helping to nurse the patients." He raked his hair back from his face. "How's Sarah?"

"Fine. I rode out on Monday to check on her. She hates being so far away. But she's safer out there than here."

"I wish she wasn't alone."

"So do I."

"I tried to get Grandpa to go out to stay with her, but he was afraid he might take sickness with him."

"He's not sick, is he?"

"No. He seems fine. I've only talked to him like this." Tom motioned at the distance between them. "But he looks okay."

"You don't."

With a grunt of acknowledgement, Tom took a step backward, his body already starting to turn. "I'd better get back to our patients."

It was the silence that Jeremiah noticed after the door closed behind Tom. The whole town seemed to hold its breath. No one walked along the street. There wasn't even a breeze to rustle the bare branches of the trees or stir the brown grass.

"Our Father is watching over us." Sarah's words whispered in his memory, as they had often over the past week. *"I trust Him to care for me. And for you."*

Trust.

The word had repeated in his heart again and again for weeks, long before influenza had arrived in Boulder Creek. One minute he was ready to trust God for his future, the next he wasn't. Yet he knew, somewhere deep in his soul, that true happiness would elude him unless he surrendered.

He looked toward the heavens, to the expanse of blue. *Surrender what?*

But he knew. Deep down he knew. Surrender his anger. Surrender his guilt. Surrender resentment and blame. Surrender his need to control.

Surrender Sarah.

A chill wrapped around his heart.

No. That was something he couldn't do. Wouldn't do.

Eyes locked on the ground, Jeremiah left the schoolyard and continued down North Street. He didn't realize his destination was the McNeal home until he found himself knocking on the door. He stepped back onto the walk before Hank could answer.

"Jeremiah." The older man smiled. "Good to see you. You're well, I take it."

"Yes, sir. I'm well."

"And Sarah?"

"She's well too. And trying not to worry about you and Tom."

"And you." Hank rubbed his jaw. "Any trouble in town?"

"No, sir. Chad's got it all under control. Most of the loggers have moved on, and others are avoiding Boulder Creek for now. The saloon is almost as quiet as the rest of town."

It occurred to him why he'd come to see Hank. It wasn't to ask if he was well or to report that Sarah was all right. He'd come to ask about the older man's faith. About how he'd suffered difficult things—hardships in his youth, the deaths of his son and daughter-in-law, the loss of his wife of many years —without losing his trust in God. How did a man trust? How did a man let go and trust in Someone beyond himself? But before he could voice his questions, Hank's gaze moved beyond Jeremiah.

"Doc," Hank said, "what is it?"

Jeremiah turned.

Doc Varney stood in the street, looking haggard and rumpled. "It's Tom."

That chill returned to Jeremiah's chest.

"He's taken ill."

Jeremiah glanced behind him in time to see Hank step onto the stoop.

"I must go to him," Hank said.

"No." Doc shook his head. "No, I've got volunteers.

Younger, healthy people. You need to steer clear. We'll manage."

Sarah would want to come to help. The instant she learned about Tom, she would come into town. Determination rose in Jeremiah. She mustn't learn about it. He couldn't let her know.

STANDING IN THE DOORWAY, SARAH WATCHED THE ROCKING D cowboy ride away. But as soon as Carter Simpson—Tom's boyhood friend—was out of sight, she sprang into action. Tom was sick, and she had to get to him.

Jeremiah should have been the one to tell her, but he hadn't ridden out to the farm today as expected. Afternoon shadows were long, and he still hadn't come. He wouldn't come, she suspected, because he didn't want to tell her about her brother.

Anger coiled in her belly. What else hadn't he told her? Was Grandpa sick too? She wasn't a child. She was Jeremiah's wife. Whether or not he loved her, she didn't deserve to be ignored. She'd been patient. She'd loved him in every way she knew how. She'd tried to honor and obey him too, just as she'd vowed on their wedding day.

But this was too much.

Carter had promised to return to feed and water Ember and her foal as well as the chickens for as long as Sarah was away. He would have cared for Bandit, too, but she couldn't bear to leave the puppy behind. And so, once her carpetbag was packed and the black gelding saddled and bridled, Sarah put Bandit into a second carpetbag and climbed aboard the horse. She nudged the gelding into a trot as soon as they were on the road. The big horse had a jarring gait, and Sarah felt like a rag doll, flopping about, her teeth rattling as she gripped the saddle horn with both hands.

Only when Boulder Creek came into view did Sarah pull back on the reins, slowing the horse to a walk. A sigh of relief escaped her lips. But her breath caught when she saw Main Street, empty of horses and wagons. Not a soul in sight. Like a ghost town. Eerie and silent. Her anger had dissipated during the lengthy ride. It was replaced now by dread.

At the school, she dismounted and tied the horse to the hitching rail. Afterward, she freed Bandit from the carpetbag but carried the puppy close to her body as she walked toward the steps.

Please let Tom be all right. He's so young. His future is before him.

With the opening of the door, the silence of the town behind her was replaced with sounds of coughing and low moans that filled the schoolroom. Cots and tick mattresses lined the walls on both sides of the room. Desks had been pushed together in a far corner. Doc Varney leaned over one patient, listening to the man's chest with a stethoscope. Two women—one young, one older—tended to other patients. But Sarah didn't even register who they were. She needed to see Tom. She'd come for her brother.

"Sarah."

She looked in Doc's direction a second time.

"What are you doing here?"

"I came to take care of Tom."

Doc stepped toward her. "Does Jeremiah know?"

"Not yet." She stiffened her spine, and with her eyes she told him it didn't matter if her husband knew it or not. She was here to stay.

The doctor gave a slight shake of his head before looking toward the last bed on the left. He didn't have to say anything before she moved in that direction. Her pulse quickened as she neared the cot.

Tom's face was pasty white, his eyes closed, his forehead creased with a frown.

"Tom?" She knelt beside the cot.

He murmured but didn't look at her.

"I don't think he really hears us."

Sarah looked up at the girl who'd come to stand on the opposite side of the bed.

"I'm Fanny."

"Fanny Adams?" Sarah knew at once that she'd been wrong to believe the romance had fizzled. Tom hadn't forgotten this girl nor had she forgotten him.

"Yes," Fanny answered as she lowered to her knees opposite Sarah. Her gaze went to Tom's face. "His fever has been high for most of the day." She tugged the top blanket closer to Tom's chin.

"Did you come to help care for him?"

Fanny looked at her again. "No. I've been here since they brought the first sick folk to the school. Doc and Tom needed help. I knew I could do whatever they needed so I offered."

"That was good of you." Sarah frowned. "Why haven't we met before?"

Fanny looked surprised by the question. "Tom didn't tell you?"

"Tell me what?"

"I worked at the Pony Saloon up until about two months ago. I don't reckon you know many of the girls there."

Sarah shook her head.

"After Deputy West helped me out of...out of a bad situation at the saloon, I went to work at the boarding house. Mrs. Tomkin's been real kind to me."

Sarah suspected Fanny could have added that Mrs. Tomkin

had been the exception to the rule. Worse, she suspected Tom hadn't told her more about Fanny because he'd feared she might not be very welcoming either. Would he have been right?

Other questions followed that one. What bad situation? What had Jeremiah done for Fanny? Why had he never mentioned it? And how angry would he be when he learned she'd come to town to care for her brother?

Tom muttered something as he rolled his head from side to side on the pillow.

Before Sarah could react, Fanny placed a hand on his forehead. "He's burning up." The girl rose. "I'll get him some cool water and a cloth."

CHAPTER

THIRTY-SIX

D usk settled over Boulder Creek as Jeremiah followed the
boardwalk through the center of town. There were a
few men inside the Pony Saloon, but Zoe's Restaurant stood
dark and empty. The quiet of the town unsettled him, even
after a full week of it. It felt even more oppressive tonight.
Probably because there'd been two more deaths reported. An
older man and his wife had been discovered by their daughter
in their home just east of town.

He stopped outside his brother's shop. Looking up at the
second story window, he wondered how Warren was doing in
Boise. Was the partnership going well? Did he have any regrets
about the move? Had the influenza reached the capital city?
Was he well?

With a shake of his head, he began the return walk through
town. Shadows had grown deeper by this time, and lights had
begun to appear in windows of homes and in the hotel and
boarding house.

"Easy, boy."

Jeremiah looked in the direction of the voice. A tall man—

he suspected it was Chad Turner's son—was leading a horse toward the corral next to the livery barn.

"Brad? Is that you?"

The younger man turned. "It's me."

Jeremiah headed toward him. "Quiet night."

"Sure is."

"Everyone well at your house?"

"Yes, sir. Wife and baby are fine. Thanks be to God."

Jeremiah stopped well back of Brad and the horse, but he was close enough, despite the encroaching darkness, that he recognized the animal. It was *his* horse. The big black he'd bought to pull the plow.

Brad led the horse into the corral and set him free. "Couldn't leave this guy tied outside the school all night."

The school?

"I guess you would've got to him eventually, but I figure you and Dad have enough to do, what with worrying about folks taking sick right and left."

He shook his head.

"With Tom down, your wife's hands were sure needed. Doc said she's been a godsend."

He'd known, of course. The moment he recognized the horse, he'd known that Sarah had come to town. "Thanks for seeing to him. I appreciate it." He turned and strode away.

Following Doc Varney's advice, Jeremiah had stayed out of the schoolhouse for the past week. He'd done his talking to those inside from the yard, reporting and receiving information at a distance. He'd brought blankets and pillows and left them on the stoop. But now Sarah was inside that building, exposing herself.

"I told her not to come to town," he muttered as he approached the school. "I told her it wasn't safe. Why didn't she do what I told her to do?"

Why can't you trust?

His chest tightened, and he stopped walking.

Without trust in God, you have nothing.

Clarity struck. Like a flash of lightning. Like a bolt from the blue. Standing there on the boardwalk in the gathering night, he knew what God wanted from him. He had to give up trying to control everything. He had to surrender to the will of God, whatever that might be. Before he could be free, be happy, be content, he had to open his hands and offer up whatever he held so tightly.

Revelation. Wasn't that what the preachers called it? A divinely revealed truth. That's what this moment was.

And another thing. He loved Sarah. Loved her more than he'd thought possible. He wanted a future with her. He wanted children with her. Loving came with risk, but not to love was not to live. He wanted to live.

He looked up at the sky where stars twinkled against the dark expanse. "I surrender," he whispered. "I'm Yours." He paused, then added, "She's Yours and we're Yours. From now on."

EXHAUSTION WEIGHED ON SARAH'S SHOULDERS AS SHE CARRIED A bowl of fresh water to Nellie Jacobs's bedside. The youngest daughter of the pastor had been brought to the school a couple of hours before. Like others in the room, her fever was high and her breathing shallow.

Sarah knelt beside the cot, then dampened a cloth in the bowl of water. After wringing it out, she bathed the young girl's face. "It's all right, Nellie," she crooned. "You're going to be fine."

A hand alighted on her shoulder, and she looked up into Doc Varney's face.

"Your husband's at the door," he said.

She'd wondered how long it would be before Jeremiah learned she was at the school. After nodding to the doctor, she placed the cloth on Nellie's forehead, then rose. Squaring her shoulders as if for battle—as she feared it would be—she walked toward the entrance, picking up an oil lamp from a table near the door.

Jeremiah stood at the bottom of the steps. Light from the lamp spilled onto his face. She'd expected to see a flash of anger in his eyes, but she saw only compassion there.

"How's Tom?" His voice was low and gentle.

"He's resting a little better now. His fever's come down some." She drew a breath. "Doc says he should recover. No need to fear the worst."

"I'm glad. I'll let Hank know."

"I...I'm sorry I came without telling you. When I heard Tom was sick—"

"I'm sorry I told you you couldn't come to help. I had no right—if that's what you felt called to do."

The words caught her by surprise.

"Sarah, there's a lot I need to say to you. This isn't the place or time for most of it. But this I can say. I'm trusting God to care for you. For me. For us."

Her heart fluttered, and she took a step forward. "Jeremiah."

He reached out a hand. To stop her approach or because he wished to touch her? "You've shown me how to trust from the very start, Sarah, but I've resisted. I didn't want to lose the control I thought I had. But control's an illusion. I realized that a little while ago. I'm sorry it took me so long."

She smiled.

"I love you, Sarah West. I've been wrong not to tell you that, too."

Unshed tears made his image waver. "And I love you." Only wanting to protect him kept her from throwing herself into his arms.

It seemed Jeremiah had the same thought. "Doc would have my hide if I came and held you right now. He'd talk about infection and all that."

"I know."

"But when this sickness passes and the town's back to normal, I'm going to hold you so tight you'll be afraid I'll never let go."

She laughed softly as she brushed away the tears with her free hand. "I think I'll like that, Jeremiah. In fact, I know I will."

EPILOGUE

The late September sun rested like a giant orange ball atop the western mountain peaks, casting long shadows across the valley floor. The evening air cooled quickly, and a gentle breeze carried with it the fragrance of autumn.

Wearing the straw hat Jeremiah had given her—a late birthday present, he'd called it—and wrapped in a shawl, Sarah stood in the barnyard, watching the sun set and marveling at its beauty. She heard the shrill whinny of Ember's filly and turned to watch Little Blaze race across the enclosed pasture toward her dam. In the neighboring pasture, the new milk cow and her calf grazed peacefully.

Sarah set her hands over the rounding of her belly. In a few months, there would be one more blessing to add to all the ones already surrounding her. Their child was due to be born in December. A Christmas baby, if Doc Varney was right. Joy flooded through her in expectation.

The barn door moaned as it swung closed, drawing Sarah's gaze across the yard to where Jeremiah stood.

He looked different from the man who'd returned to

Boulder Creek the previous December. His face had been bronzed by the summer sun. His muscles had been honed and his hands calloused from difficult labor. But what was truly different was something that came from within.

Jeremiah West was at peace—with himself and with God.

"How's everyone in town?" she asked.

"Good. I had a long talk with your grandfather and Fanny. They had a letter from Tom today."

"Nothing for me?"

"Yes." He grinned, pulling an envelope from his pocket. "He wrote to you too."

"I don't know why I care. He'll only ask about Fanny." She laughed softly. "I hope he's paying attention to his studies and not mooning about her all the time."

Jeremiah walked toward her. "I'd moon about you if a couple thousand miles were between us."

His words sent joy spiraling through her.

"He'll be home again in the summer for their wedding, and in the meantime, Hank's got Fanny's company."

"She's a special girl. I'm glad for Tom. I'm glad for them both."

"Me too." He stopped in front of her, his right hand covering both of hers on her belly. "How's the little one?"

"Active."

They turned in unison, and Jeremiah placed his arm around her shoulders as they watched the sun slip the rest of the way behind the mountains.

"I talked to Norman Henderson while I was in town. He says our crops should get the best prices farmers have had in years. We'll be able to make some improvements around here in the spring."

"This place is next to perfect as it is."

Jeremiah chuckled. "You would say that." He leaned close and kissed her forehead.

She closed her eyes as she laid her head against his shoulder, remembering when she'd dreamed of finding her heart's desire in Philadelphia or New York, London or Paris. Remembering when she'd dreamed of a mysterious European count riding in on a prancing horse. And remembering when she'd discovered that everything she wanted, all she ever dreamed, could be found in this man who stood at her side.

She sighed as he pulled her into a tight embrace, kissing her, slow and deep.

No mysterious count could hold a candle to Jeremiah West when it came to making dreams come true.

IF YOU ENJOYED THIS BOOK...
PLEASE TAKE A MOMENT TO LEAVE A REVIEW

Word of mouth is so important for authors today. It would mean so much to me, if you enjoyed *All She Ever Dreamed*, if you would leave a review for it. Even just a few words can make a difference. Here are just three suggested sites where you can leave a review:

Amazon

Goodreads

BookBub

YOU MIGHT ALSO LIKE . .

.

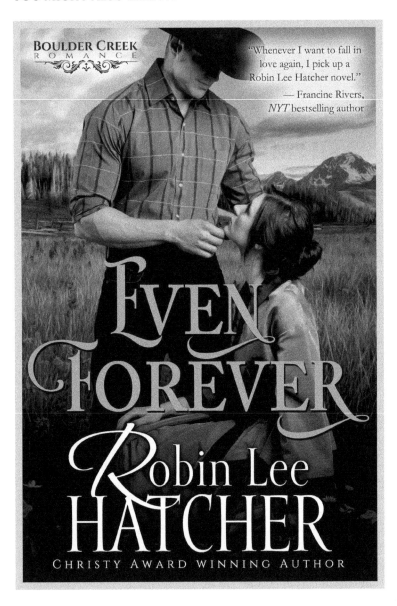

Even Forever
Boulder Creek Romance #1

The last thing Rosalie Tomkin wants is another man trying to control her life.

Rosalie's abusive jailbird father and her ne'er-do-well brother have cured her of that. Not even the wealthy visitor staying in her beleaguered mother's boarding house can tempt her. She plans to leave Boulder Creek as soon as she can scrape together the funds to do so, and when she does, she won't ever look back.

Michael Randolph is in a high-stakes competition for the family business and intends to beat his half-brother, no matter what. So when an innocent encounter with Rosalie threatens to cost him everything he hopes to achieve, he's willing to pay the price demanded by her no-good father. Even if it means marrying a damsel in distress.

Strangers placed in an impossible position, Michael and Rosalie can agree on one thing. Neither of them wants to stay together any longer than they must. What they don't know is that fate might have a better future in store for them than either could imagine.

EVEN FOREVER

CHAPTER ONE

Boulder Creek, Idaho Territory
May 1890

"Your pa's coming home."

The soup ladle dropped from Rosalie Tomkin's hand into the kettle, splashing an ugly stain onto her apron. She closed her eyes and drew in a deep breath, hoping against hope that when she opened them she would find she'd only imagined her mother's words. But when she looked, she still stood before the stove in the kitchen of the Crescent Valley Room and Board.

Rosalie turned around. Her heart raced and an odd buzzing sounded in her ears. She felt choked by the icy panic swelling inside of her. "He's coming *here*?" Her voice was little more than a whisper.

Her ma, Virginia Tomkin, nodded as she lifted the letter in one hand.

It can't be true. It can't be true. "When?"

"Couple weeks, according to his letter. Doesn't say exactly when they let him out, just when he should get to Boulder Creek."

Rosalie shook her head, trying to clear her thoughts. "But why's he coming *here*?"

"Where else is he to go? He lost the saloon while he was in prison. Besides, for all he's done, this *is* still his home ... and I'm still his wife."

Rosalie's voice sharpened. "This was *never* a home, not as long as he was in it. Ma, you can't let him come back. You *can't*."

Ma lifted her shoulders in a helpless gesture. "For better or worse, I'm his wife. That's the vow I took when I married him. He's got a right to come back, if that's what he wants. I can't rightly stop him."

Rosalie opened her mouth to protest again, then turned toward the stove. If her ma had wanted to change her life, she would have done it long before now. She would have done it the first time her husband hit her. Or she would have done it the first time he struck one of their children.

No, there was nothing Rosalie could do to keep her pa from coming back to Boulder Creek and resuming his life in the boarding house. And once he was there, there would be nothing she could do to keep him from hurting Ma—or from hurting *her*.

She closed her eyes as her hands clenched against her stomach. Pa was coming back. Pa was going to move into the boarding house and stay in the room next to her own. And then he would drink, and when he got drunk, he would strike out at them in the black rages Rosalie remembered all too well. Mostly he would hit Ma. He would hit her until she had to hide in the house so nobody would see her black eyes or her swollen lips. There wouldn't be anything Rosalie could do about it. Everything would be the way it used to be, before he went away. Everything would be the same.

Rosalie stiffened her spine and opened her eyes. No, it wouldn't be the same. She was older now. She wouldn't let him hurt Ma, and she wasn't going to let him hurt her either. Never again. Not ever again.

She turned to face Ma a second time. "I've got almost forty-five dollars saved from working at the restaurant. We could leave Boulder Creek. We could go to San Francisco ... or as far as it'll take us. I could find work. I'd take care of you, Ma."

Ma's smile was bittersweet. "You shouldn't ought to have to take care of your ma. You're too young to have such worries."

"I'm not a child anymore. I'm going on nineteen. Say you'll come with me."

"I can't go, Rosalie."

"Then I'll go alone."

"Rosalie—"

"I can't stay, Ma. I hate what he did to you and to me and to..." She felt the old sickness churning in her stomach as a vision of the burning sawmill sprang into her mind. But Rosalie had never told anyone what she suspected her pa had done the day he left Boulder Creek nearly a decade ago, and so she stopped herself before she could speak those suspicions aloud.

Ma's shoulders sagged. "If you feel you have to go, I'll give you what money I can spare."

"You haven't anything to spare." Rosalie knew that whatever profit the boarding house made, her brother, Mark, drank up at the Pony Saloon. "We don't have any boarders now. You'll need anything you have to see you through." She untied her apron as she spoke, hanging it on a peg near the stove. "I'd better get ready for work." She headed toward the hall.

"Rosalie?"

She stopped and glanced over her shoulder.

"When will you leave?"

"Before he gets here. On the next stage."

"So soon?"

"I've got to, Ma."

Ma nodded in resignation. "I'll miss you, Rosalie."

"I'll miss you, too."

Michael Randolph stopped his horse and stared down the lone street of Boulder Creek. He'd known it wasn't a city like Denver or San Francisco, but he'd hoped it would be bigger than the small town that lay before him.

He nudged the roan gelding with his boot heels and started down the street, his eyes perusing each building, making note of things most folks wouldn't see. For instance, though it had a fresh coat of paint, the Barber Mercantile had been around longer than the other buildings in town, probably twelve to fifteen years longer. The First Bank of Boulder Creek, in contrast, hadn't been built more than two years ago, judging by the appearance of the red brick walls.

Besides the bank and general store, there were the usual businesses that made up small towns across the West—a church, a school, a livery and blacksmith shop, restaurant, saloon, barber shop and bath house, post office, and a jail. Michael had seen the like in a hundred different places. What was missing, of course, was a hotel.

And that was why Michael Randolph had come to Boulder Creek.

John Thomas must be getting senile to send me to a town like this.

John Thomas Randolph had never operated a hotel in any but the biggest cities in America. Michael's father had taught him everything about building and running a hotel in cities like San Francisco, Denver, Chicago, and New York. How was he supposed to run a profitable hotel in a backwater burg like this?

His mouth thinned.

Of course, that was no doubt *why* John Thomas had chosen Boulder Creek. Because Michael would have to prove himself in unfamiliar territory.

"Since you and Dillon don't seem inclined to agree on anything," his father had announced several months ago, "there's only one thing for me to do. I'll leave Palace Hotels to one of you when I'm gone. It'll be up to you to prove who that one will be."

The surprise and betrayal Michael had felt then was just as strong today. He shouldn't have to prove himself. He'd known since the time he was a small boy that the business would be his. It should be his without question. He was the oldest Randolph son as well as the legitimate heir. Dillon, while indisputably John Thomas's son, had no right to any part of Palace Hotels.

Michael shoved those thoughts from his mind. He had no time to examine old wounds that continued to fester. He was in Boulder Creek to win what was rightfully his, and unless he wanted to lose the management and eventual ownership of Palace Hotels to his half-brother, he'd better set his plans in motion. He would need a place to stay, but before that he wanted something to eat. He stopped his horse in front of a wooden building with a sign that identified it as Zoe's Restaurant.

Dismounting, he brushed the trail dust from his trousers and the sleeves of his shirt, then stepped onto the boardwalk and entered the establishment. Delicious odors greeted him, and his stomach growled in response. The place was empty of customers. If it weren't for the sounds and smells coming from the kitchen, he would wonder if the restaurant was open for business. Certainly no one bothered to answer the bells that jingled when he opened the door.

He selected a table against a wall, with a view of both the front door and the entrance to the kitchen, and sat down, placing his hat on one of the other chairs. He was untroubled by the wait. His stepmother said that Michael had the patience of Job. She also said he had the stubbornness of a mule. He was willing to act or wait, whichever was most beneficial. He was hungry now, so he waited.

About five minutes later, the bells jingled again as the front door of the restaurant swung inward, and a young woman hurried through the opening. Michael had a quick impression of shiny, chestnut colored hair swept smoothly up from her neck, gathered in a bun atop her head, and of a pleasingly female figure compacted into a body barely five feet tall.

She stopped short when she saw him.

"Rosalie, is that you?" a voice called from the kitchen.

She looked away from him. "Yes, it's me, Mrs. Paddock."

A middle-aged woman came out of the kitchen. Michael supposed she could be the Zoe of Zoe's Restaurant as well as the young woman's Mrs. Paddock. "I was just—" Her words broke off when she noticed Michael. "Oh, dear. I didn't know we had a customer."

"No trouble, ma'am." He nodded in her direction. "I didn't mind the wait."

"Rosalie, will you take the gentleman's order?" Mrs. Paddock turned away. "I've got chickens roasting."

Michael watched as Rosalie followed the woman through the swinging door, reappearing a moment later wearing a crisp white apron over her simple blue blouse and skirt. A white cap now covered much of her dark hair. She carried a small paper tablet in her left hand and a pencil in her right.

She crossed the room, stopping on the opposite side of the table from him. "What would you like, sir?" She pointed toward the wall near the entrance.

Her eyes weren't brown, he realized. They were hazel, the dark centers flecked with gold. She was young, but something about her eyes made her seem older, wiser, a little sad. He wondered why.

"Sir?"

"Sorry." He turned his gaze in the direction she'd pointed. Written on a blackboard in precise letters was the menu for the day. He considered his choices. "I'll have the corn-dodgers, chicken-fixins, and coffee."

Rosalie slipped the pencil into the pocket of her apron. "I'll bring your coffee right out." With that, she disappeared into the kitchen.

Two men entered the restaurant soon after. One was dressed in a business suit and bow tie, the other in denim trousers and a vest with a badge pinned to it. There was a look about the first man that almost shouted "Banker." Michael knew it was wise to get on good terms with the town financier as soon as possible. Such men tended to wield a strong voice in any community. Folks listened to their advice as if it were gospel. The second man was obviously the sheriff. He had steel gray hair and eyes to match and was built like a grizzly bear. When the sheriff looked his way, Michael nodded, silently admitting he was a stranger in town.

By the time the men were settled at a table, two more customers arrived, an older couple who reminded Michael of the nursery rhyme about Jack Sprat and his wife. The man was bean pole thin with a shiny bald head, the woman merrily plump with thick gray hair. They, too, glanced his way. The woman's eyes sparkled with curiosity, as if to say, *We don't get many strangers in Boulder Creek.* As with the sheriff, Michael acknowledged her frank appraisal with a slight nod.

Just then, the waitress entered the dining room, carrying Michael's cup of coffee.

"Afternoon, Rosalie," the other woman called.

Rosalie smiled. "Afternoon, Mrs. Barber, Mr. Barber." She set Michael's coffee on the table, then headed toward her other customers. "Sheriff, Mr. Stanley." She pulled her small tablet and pencil from the pocket of her apron. "What can I get for you today? Mrs. Paddock's got some mighty good chicken-fixins ready, and there's beef steak available. She's also baked up some cider cakes and cherry pies."

Michael sipped his coffee, observing the waitress as she took each of their orders. Now that he wasn't distracted by the sorrow he'd read in her eyes, he could study the rest of her appearance. He found it much to his liking. She was sweetly pretty with a heart-shaped face and dimples that appeared whenever she smiled. Her mouth was small and pink, her nose dainty. Long lashes—the same dark chestnut color as her hair—framed her expressive eyes.

He lowered his gaze. He didn't feel guilty for noticing the pretty waitress, but he wondered if he should. He'd kept company with Louise Overhart for more than a year, and all of their friends and acquaintances expected them to marry. Coming from one of San Francisco's most distinguished families, Louise was beautiful, sophisticated, and intelligent. There was no reason why he shouldn't marry her, yet he felt no urgency to do so.

He looked up again, gazing across the restaurant at the

waitress called Rosalie. What would it be like to be married to someone like her instead? The question made him think of home cooked suppers and bedroom slippers and long nights spent nestled in a featherbed in a house in a small town like Boulder Creek.

But those things weren't for Michael Randolph. He thrived on the bustle of the big city. He loved the challenge of business. He enjoyed nothing more than a night at the theater or a brutal game of cards with the men at his club.

He wasn't interested in a small town waitress with sad eyes. And he never would be.

"Who's the stranger?" Zoe asked when Rosalie entered the kitchen, bringing more orders with her.

"I didn't ask. He didn't say." Rosalie glanced down at her tablet. "I need one beef stew, an order of chicken-fixins, corn-dodgers, and a slice of cherry pie, and two orders of ham, mashed potatoes, and slaw." She dropped the tablet into her pocket. "I'll serve the coffee."

Rosalie wasn't as disinterested in the stranger's identity as she pretended. Outsiders passed through Boulder Creek on their way to the mining areas or the logging camps. Others came looking for land with intentions of settling in this valley or the next one over. But few of them were as handsome or as well-dressed as this particular traveler, and she couldn't help wondering what had brought him to there.

As she carried a tray into the dining room, Rosalie cast a surreptitious glance in the stranger's direction. She wasn't mistaken about his good looks. He had hair the color of spun gold, and his eyes were the blue of a summer sky. His masculine features seemed nothing short of perfect, from his straight nose, to his firm mouth, to his beardless jaw. His profile spoke of power and confidence, yet she sensed a measure of gentleness beneath the surface.

Looking at him, she was reminded of the books she'd read in school, her studies of Greek gods of mythology or romantic medieval knights from ancient poetry. But she'd never thought they could be real until she saw this man.

He looked up and their gazes met. Rosalie glanced away, but not before she felt heat rise in her cheeks.

"You seem to have an admirer," Emma Barber said softly as Rosalie set two cups of coffee on the table. "Who is he?"

"I don't know. I never saw him before."

"Sam, you know who he is?" Emma asked.

Her husband looked across the room, then back at Emma. "Nope." He picked up his coffee and blew on the steamy hot liquid.

"New in town," Emma continued, undeterred by her husband's lack of interest. "I wonder if he's come to stay."

Rosalie had wondered the same thing but wasn't about to admit it. Besides, it didn't matter. She wouldn't be around more than a few days. What did she care if this stranger stayed? She was leaving Boulder Creek.

She felt a tiny flutter in her stomach, a niggle of fear along her spine. She couldn't remember living anywhere but here. What would it be like, out there on her own?

Silently, she set the other two cups of coffee in front of the sheriff and Vince Stanley, then returned to the kitchen to help Zoe, trying not to think about how frightening it might be to leave Boulder Creek.

Still, she knew it would be worse to stay, now that Pa was coming back.

Not a scrap of food remained on Michael's dinner plate when the woman at the next table—Mrs. Barber, he remembered Rosalie calling her—caught his eye.

She smiled and said, "You're new to Boulder Creek."

He nodded as he rose from his chair and picked up his hat. "Yes, ma'am." He pulled some coins from his pocket and left the payment for his meal beside his empty plate.

"Are you settling in the area?"

"I'm here on business." He walked toward her table. Turning his eyes on her husband, he held out his hand and said, "I'm Michael Randolph."

"Sam Barber." The men shook hands. "This here is my wife, Emma."

"I'm pleased to meet you both." He offered a polite bow. "Perhaps you can help me. I need a place to stay. Are there any rooms for rent in Boulder Creek?"

"There's the boarding house down near the church. Crescent Valley Room and Board. Mrs. Tomkin's rates are reasonable, and she's a good cook. You'll be comfortable there."

"Tomkin, did you say?"

"Yes, Virginia Tomkin. She's run the place for more than ten years now. Used to be called Tomkin's Rooming House, but when we started getting so many newcomers to the valley, Virginia did some fixing up and adding on and changed the name. You can't miss it." She pointed down the street toward the west end of town. "Big, two-story place. There's a sign on the porch."

"Much obliged." Michael placed his black Stetson over his hair, then touched the brim and nodded before turning and leaving the restaurant.

ABOUT THE AUTHOR

Robin Lee Hatcher is the best-selling author of over 85 books with over five million copies in print. Her well-drawn characters and heartwarming stories of faith, courage, and love have earned her both critical acclaim and the devotion of readers. Her numerous awards include the Christy Award for Excellence in Christian Fiction, the RITA® Award for Best Inspirational Romance, Romantic Times Career Achievement Awards for Americana Romance and for Inspirational Fiction, the Carol Award, the 2011 Idahope Writer of the Year, and Lifetime Achievement Awards from both Romance Writers of America® (2001) and American Christian Fiction Writers (2014). *Catching Katie* was named one of the Best Books of 2004 by the Library Journal.

When not writing, Robin enjoys being with her family, spending time in the beautiful Idaho outdoors, Bible art journaling, reading books that make her cry, watching romantic movies, and decorative planning. A mother and grandmother, Robin makes her home on the outskirts of Boise, sharing it with a demanding Papillon dog and a persnickety tuxedo cat.

Learn more about Robin and her books by visiting her website at https://robinleehatcher.com

You can also find out more by joining her in the following ways:

Goodreads | Bookbub | Newsletter sign-up

Also by Robin Lee Hatcher

Stand Alone Titles

Like the Wind

I'll Be Seeing You

Make You Feel My Love

An Idaho Christmas

Here in Hart's Crossing

The Victory Club

Beyond the Shadows

Catching Katie

Whispers From Yesterday

The Shepherd's Voice

Ribbon of Years

Firstborn

The Forgiving Hour

Heart Rings

A Wish and a Prayer

When Love Blooms

A Carol for Christmas

Return to Me

Loving Libby

Wagered Heart

The Perfect Life

Speak to Me of Love

Trouble in Paradise

Another Chance to Love You

Bundle of Joy

Boulder Creek Romance

Even Forever

All She Ever Dreamed

The Coming to America

Dear Lady

Patterns of Love

In His Arms

Promised to Me

Where the Heart Lives

Belonging

Betrayal

Beloved

Books set in Kings Meadow

A Promise Kept

Love Without End

Whenever You Come Around

I Hope You Dance

Keeper of the Stars

Books set in Thunder Creek

You'll Think of Me

You're Gonna Love Me

The Sisters of Bethlehem Springs

A Vote of Confidence

Fit to Be Tied

A Matter of Character

Legacy of Faith series

Who I am With You

Cross My Heart

How Sweet It Is

For a full list of books, visit www.robinleehatcher.com